T0137497

Other Books Written by Connie Squiers

The Copper Colt

Hannah's Chance

Spirit's Legacy

Choctaw

Shady Springs Ranch

Shadow

Dakota

Montana Mustang

Carolina Dream

Kat's Queen

BLACK JAZZ

Julie's Beautiful Friesian Colt

Connie Squiers

WESTBOW
P R E S S®
A DIVISION OF THOMAS NELSON
& ZONDERVAN

Copyright © 2019 Connie Squiers.

All rights reserved. No part of this book may be used or reproduced by any means, graphic, electronic, or mechanical, including photocopying, recording, taping or by any information storage retrieval system without the written permission of the author except in the case of brief quotations embodied in critical articles and reviews.

WestBow Press books may be ordered through booksellers or by contacting:

WestBow Press
A Division of Thomas Nelson & Zondervan
1663 Liberty Drive
Bloomington, IN 47403
www.westbowpress.com
1 (866) 928-1240

Because of the dynamic nature of the Internet, any web addresses or links contained in this book may have changed since publication and may no longer be valid. The views expressed in this work are solely those of the author and do not necessarily reflect the views of the publisher, and the publisher hereby disclaims any responsibility for them.

Any people depicted in stock imagery provided by Getty Images are models, and such images are being used for illustrative purposes only. Certain stock imagery © Getty Images.

ISBN: 978-1-9736-7973-8 (sc)
ISBN: 978-1-9736-7972-1 (hc)
ISBN: 978-1-9736-7974-5 (e)

Library of Congress Control Number: 2019918212

Print information available on the last page.

WestBow Press rev. date: 11/21/2019

CONTENTS

DEDICATED

to my two sons,
Billy Austin Stalnaker and Daniel Scott Squiers;
and to my very special sister,
Janice Lynn Hopkins

A special thanks to Rob Burke of Feather'd Hoof
Farm and Stunning Steed Photography for permission
to use the beautiful photograph of Monarch T.
It has been a great inspiration to me while writing this book.
They can be reached at http://featherdhooffarm.com and
stunningsteeds.com took the beautiful picture on the cover.

CHAPTER 1
Tragedy Strikes

AUNT FRAN PATTED the seat next to her, "Julie, sweetheart, come sit down for a minute."

As Julie slowly sat down, she thought, *what can it be now? Every time she uses that tone of voice, it's been bad news.* Her heart beat faster as she waited.

Aunt Fran continued in a sugary sweet voice. "You know Jim and I love you, don't you?"

Julie looked down and nodded yes. She trembled, waiting. She knew nothing could be worse than last month when her aunt told her both her parents had been killed in a plane crash. That memory flashed before her eyes, and she held her breath. The pain of remembering was terrible.

"I'm glad you know we care, because what I am going to tell you is difficult." Julie panicked and started to get up to leave the room. Her aunt stopped her, "Sit down and listen, Julie. I'll make this as quick and as painless as possible."

Julie sat back down, "You *are* aware your Uncle Jim has been very sick lately and has been unable to work. His doctors say his illness could turn into a permanent disability, which means our money is very limited and will be even more so in the future." She cleared her throat. "We've made arrangements for you to live somewhere else until we get on our feet again."

Julie's eyes opened wide, not believing what she was hearing. Her aunt continued, "As you can imagine, it's very difficult to take care of our needs with only me working." She paused, hoping Julie would understand without her saying anything further.

Reality slowly sank in, and she asked, "So Aunt Fran, you want me to live somewhere else?"

Her aunt hastily explained, "Well, yes, but it won't be as bad as you're making it sound."

Julie shouted, "How could it *not* be as bad as it sounds? Where? Where will I live? How can you do this to me?"

"Calm down, dear. I'm trying to tell you you'll be going to live with a relative."

Julie panicked, "Who and where? I was born and raised in Florida, and I have no kin but you."

Her aunt carefully explained, "Well, what you said isn't entirely true. Unfortunately, you would not be living in this state."

Julie wailed, "What!!! Where then?"

Her aunt spoke hesitantly, "Colorado. You'll be living in Colorado."

She violently objected, "No way! I don't know anyone in Colorado, and it snows in Colorado." She wailed, "I've never even *seen* snow!"

"Listen to me, Julie. At this point, your Uncle Mark is the only option we have. He's your only other next of kin."

Julie cried out, "I've never even heard of an Uncle Mark. No one here has ever mentioned his name. Why him?"

"He was your mom's and my older brother. He hasn't been in contact with the family for many years, probably because he's a loner."

Julie snorted, "And you think *he'd* be an appropriate person to be my guardian. Are you out of your mind?"

Fran barely stopped herself from slapping her niece for talking back, but Julie saw the hate-filled look in her eyes so she quietly responded. "Well, living with *him* will certainly be better than living here. When do I leave?"

"Fairly soon, Julie. I have no choice, and," she hesitated, "you'll have to get there by plane." She quickly explained, "I do realize your parents were killed in an airplane accident and traveling by plane will probably be disturbing to you, but I have no choice."

Julie was shaking inside but asked, "You'll be taking me out to Colorado and introduce me to this *loner*, won't you?"

Her aunt stood up in a huff. "You'll not talk to me like that, young lady, especially since I've been so good to you."

Though Julie was furious and scared, she forced herself to act calm. "You *will* be going with me, won't you?"

Her aunt sat down again and took her hand. "Julie, dear, I can't take you to Colorado myself because I can't afford to pay for a trip for two — and it goes without saying I wouldn't be able to afford my ticket back to Florida." She calmly explained, "I would have sent you by train or bus, but the companies I contacted told me if a child is less than seventeen, their rules say minors must be accompanied by an adult. However, minors your age *are* allowed travel alone on an airplane if someone meets them on the other end."

Julie sighed and asked with resignation, "When do I leave?"

Aunt Fran braced herself for more rants from her niece. "The day after tomorrow is when you leave."

Julie was now in shock and whined, "That gives me almost no time to say goodbye to my friends."

"Sorry, but I've already bought your ticket and have arranged to have your uncle meet you when you get to Denver."

CHAPTER 2
Move to Colorado

IT DIDN'T TAKE long for Julie to pack her things, because most of her clothes were for the warm Florida climate. She had a sweater or two, but they were lightweight and certainly wouldn't protect her from the cold she expected in Colorado. As she packed, she prayed, *Father, my world is upside-down. My parents are dead, and now I'm being shipped to someone I don't even know, who lives in a state that has snow. This can't be happening to me. Please help me. Amen.*

Julie dreaded the trip, because she was not only afraid of flying, but the plane was whisking her into an unknown and frightening future with a stranger. She hadn't even known she had an uncle, much less one who lived out west. If only her parents were still alive, none of this would be happening. She slept little the night before she left, and her eyes were still swollen from crying when she was dropped off at the airport.

On the plane, she was blessed to be sitting next to an older woman who reassured her it was safe to fly, because she had flown many, many miles with no problems. On takeoff, Julie gripped the armrest tightly, squeezed her eyes closed, and prayed. *Lord Jesus, please let me live through this. My aunt told me to think of this plane ride and moving to Colorado as an adventure, but I can't. I just can't. Please hold me in your arms until we land. Amen.*

Once they were at cruising altitude, Julie slowly opened her eyes and looked out the window. What a surprise! She could see the earth from the window, and it looked like a patchwork quilt, with fields like squares of different sizes and colors. The clouds below were like fluffs of white cotton, and, amazingly, she could see them from the top, not just the bottom. The sights were so breathtaking she forgot to be afraid but instead was fascinated by all she saw. The woman sitting next to her smiled and thought how wonderful it was to be sitting next to a youngster who hadn't flown before. This young girl had never seen the earth from this perspective and was fascinated by its beauty.

The Denver airport was huge and very impressive from the air. The main terminal looked like a range of mountains, or tepees, lit up from inside like beautiful lanterns against the dark night sky.

After they landed, she again felt fear. Soon she was going to meet the man who would be her guardian. What if he was mean, and she was afraid of him? She felt helpless and prayed. *Father, please make him like me and not hurt me. What if he doesn't come to the airport to get me, and I'm left alone out here in Colorado where I don't know anyone? Please* She couldn't finish the prayer. How could she tell him how she felt? Then she smiled because she remembered God already knew how she felt. He knew and loved everything about her.

When she exited the jetway after they landed, she looked around in panic. How would she know this man—this uncle she'd never heard of nor met? Then she saw a man with a rough beard holding up a sign that read, JULIE KASTING. For an instant she was relieved he was here to pick her up, but then the dread returned. She walked over to him and softly said, "I'm Julie."

He extended his hand and smiled. "And I'm Mark Hubbard. Nice to meet you, Julie." Then he took her carry-on bag and led her to baggage claim. After grabbing her suitcase off the conveyer belt, he asked her what her other bags looked like so he could pull them off too.

Defiantly, Julie looked him straight in the eye. "This is all I have."

Mark tried to hide his shock, "So the rest of your stuff is being mailed to you?"

"No, this is it. Most of my clothes would not be warm enough for Colorado, so I left them behind."

"All right then, let's get going. We have a bit of a trip ahead of us, and it's getting late."

Julie was curious. "Where do you live anyway?"

"Estes Park, which is about seventy miles from Denver."

"Why do you live out there? Why not Denver?"

Mark laughed. "Me, live in Denver? Not likely. I like the country, not the big city."

Julie started to say something else, but her uncle interrupted. "Do you always ask so many questions?"

Embarrassed, she was quiet until they arrived in Estes Park. They drove through the town, out into the country, and then turned onto a gravel drive with a large lighted sign marking the road. It simply said, ESTES PARK WILDERNESS OUTFITTERS. When Julie asked if this was where he lived, he grunted and pulled the truck up in front of a rustic lodge.

Once inside she looked around. It was large, but you could tell no woman lived there. It had no personal touches like her mom's place. Mark asked her if she was hungry, and she shook her head no. She didn't tell him she was too nervous to eat because she was afraid. He turned and headed upstairs. "Okay then, follow me, and I'll show you to your room."

She was surprised her room was so large but not surprised it lacked style. It had a double bed, a desk, a dresser, and a nightstand but no television. Was there a television downstairs? She'd find out soon enough, but tonight she just wanted to shower and go to bed.

Julie awakened to someone banging pots and pans in the kitchen. It took her a moment to remember where she was, and then the dread returned. She got up and showered, threw on a pair of jeans, then headed downstairs. She wasn't about to ask who was making all that racket, because she knew it was her Uncle Mark.

He looked over at her as she came into the kitchen, "Thought

I'd let you sleep late this morning, since you had such a long day yesterday."

When Julie glanced at the clock on the stove, it read o'clock. She thought to herself, *this is sleeping late?*

Her uncle spoke up, "As soon as we finish breakfast, we'll go out to see the animals."

Julie thought, *Oh great. We're going out to see his stinky old horses. I want to see the ocean and the beach, like we have at home. Home, that's where my heart is, and that's where I want to be.*

* * *

Mark shouted words over his shoulder as he walked briskly toward the barn. "This is Barn 1. It's where we keep our working stock—the ones we lease to outfitters who need horses and pack animals for the treks they lead into the mountains." He explained. "I know they aren't pretty animals, but they're sturdy and sure-footed. We even have a few mules in here." He stopped to scratch a mule's chin as he passed by. "This here is Turk, one of our best. He was already named when I got him, so I have no idea why they named him Turk, but he's been a great pack animal for us."

Julie followed him down the line of stalls, trying not to step in anything messy along the way. These were, after all, her favorite pink sandals. When they left Barn 1, her uncle led her to a modern steel building behind it.

Julie asked, "What's this place?"

"Barn 2, of course. This is where I keep the rest of the horses— the ones I use for our own wilderness excursions. I keep most of our breeding stock in here as well."

Julie was amazed at the difference in the two barns. The first one was old and functional, but this one looked sleek, modern, and efficient. Each stall was twelve feet square with masonry walls and had beautiful wooden sliding stall doors. Julie had a question, "I think I saw some fences beside the barn. Does each horse have a fenced yard?"

"Well, I guess you could say that, but we say there's a small paddock attached to each stall, so they can get some fresh air."

"Where do you keep their food, like hay?"

"We have a feed room at the other end of the barn. We don't keep hay in this barn, because it's too much of a fire hazard. We have another building for that."

Julie noticed an open area ahead. Before she could ask, he explained. "That section gives us a large area to wash and groom horses inside the barn. We built in floor drains to make it easier to clean the floor." He gruffly commented, "I don't know why I'm telling you all this; you don't even like horses."

Julie was too embarrassed to admit he was right. She didn't like horses because she was afraid of them. She thought they were big, strong, and unpredictable. Julie looked in each stall as they moved toward the back of the barn. She suddenly stopped and commented when they came to the last stall, "That horse looks very fat. What's the matter with it?"

"That's Shasta, and she's fat because she's pregnant, and is due to have her foal around Christmas. Even if she wasn't pregnant, she'd look out of place here, wouldn't she? She's coal black, her ears are small and alert, and her head is more delicate-looking than any of my other horses and mules, and I guess you've already noticed her long, flowing mane and tail."

Julie's uncle then reached over the stall door and patted the mare's neck. "This is one classy horse, for sure. I didn't buy her. She was given to me when my best friend moved back East to be near his grandchildren. He didn't think it'd be fair to cart her halfway across the country, because she was with foal."

Julie was amazed, "He just gave her to you?"

"Yup. I imagine after she's had her foal, and it's weaned, I can sell her. I'll probably get pretty good money for her too. Dan, my friend, left her papers with me because she's a registered Friesian."

"What's a Friesian?"

"She's one of those fancy horse breeds, and that's why she doesn't really fit in here. I'll tell you more about Friesians sometime, but right now we've got to feed and water all these beasts."

"Beasts? Why do you call them beasts?"

"I'm sort of teasing, because I love horses and always have. Why on earth would I be in this business if I didn't like horses? Even my old mules and half-breed horses are beautiful, in their own way. I like 'em all. To me, 'beasts' is an affectionate term."

Julie wrinkled her nose, "I'm sure you love them except for their smell."

"Not true. That's something I like as well, but only a horse lover would think that."

CHAPTER 3
Introduction to Horses

THE NEXT MORNING Julie grumbled as she cleaned off her new sandals. *Maybe I should wear old tennis shoes around the barn and keep these sandals for going out somewhere fancy.* Little did she know that "fancy" did not describe anything in Estes Park.

The next day was gorgeous. It was fall, and the aspen leaves were turning yellow. She thought the leaves looked like gold coins hanging on the trees. There were no aspen trees where she came from, that was for sure. Uncle Mark had awakened her at six this morning, but surprisingly, she hadn't minded. The day before she'd found a pup wandering around in Barn 1, so she had a new friend. She asked her uncle what kind of dog he was, and he just grunted, "A mutt."

Julie didn't care, because she thought he was cute, though his paws were far too large for his body. She guessed he'd probably grow up to be a very big dog. Julie knelt and looked him over. "Hey, little guy, I'm going to name you Brutus." The pup seemed to understand and started licking her face. "Whoa there, Brutus. I need to breathe, and you're not helping."

A few days later, Julie was walking through the barns and greeted several ranch hands as they went about their work. When she turned a corner, she almost ran into her uncle.

He scowled at her. "Hasn't anyone given you a job yet?" She pulled back and shook her head no. "Well, there's plenty to be done around here, so follow me."

She did as she was told.

"I normally start a new person out cleaning stalls, but I'm going to go easy on you." When they reached the tack room, he pointed to rows of bridles, saddles, and saddlebags. "I'd like you to clean those today. There's saddle soap and cloths on the shelf over there. I'll be back in a couple of hours to check on you." With that he turned and left, leaving her wide-eyed and speechless.

When he was out of sight, she said out loud, "*Me* clean saddles? I'm just a kid and not a servant." But she grabbed the saddle soap anyway and went to work, muttering the whole time about there being child labor laws, even in Colorado.

After two hours of soaping and buffing leather, she left the tack room and started exploring. She really didn't like most of the horses whose heads hung over their stall doors, but she remembered the pretty black horse she'd seen her first day. Could that have been only four days ago? It seemed like she'd been in Colorado a month.

When Julie reached the last stall, she looked in. The black horse wasn't facing the door, but seemed to be staring into a corner. How sad she looked. She tapped on the door frame and called her softly. No response. Then she started looking for a sign that would tell her this horse's name. There it was, on a plaque tacked up beside the stall door, and the letters plainly read SHASTA.

"Shasta, turn around so I can see you better. Come here, sweetheart." She thought to herself, *Me, calling a horse sweetheart. That's a first. What's the matter with me?* Slowly and awkwardly, Shasta turned around. "Come on, girl." Then the mare slowly moved toward Julie.

She thought, *Now what should I do?* Julie held out her hand, flat like she'd been told to do, because she didn't want the horse to bite her. She felt the mare's warm breath on her palm and then a puff of air as Shasta sniffed, taking in her scent. *This hasn't been too hard, and the horse seems to like me. I wonder what its nose feels like.* A moment later she found out and was surprised. It was as soft as velvet. Once she realized Shasta was just sniffing her hand and not biting her, she looked into the horse's eyes. Again, she was surprised. They were warm, curious, and friendly. She thought, *Whoa! How cool is this!* She was touching a horse and actually liking it!

Julie wanted to put her hand on Shasta's neck, just to see what it felt like but thought touching her muzzle was enough for one visit. She would come back in a couple of hours, and maybe the mare would let her touch her again. Julie's next hours were filled with work on the tack and with thinking about Shasta.

She was daydreaming when her uncle suddenly appeared at the door.

"Well, it looks like you're making progress. Would you like to take a break and walk along some of the fence line with me after lunch? We've got to check the fences before the snow comes, so our animals can't get off the property. Plus, it'll give you a chance to see the land around here."

As they left the lodge and headed out, Mark looked down and grinned. "I see you're not wearing sandals today. How'd they work for you the other day?"

Julie thought, *Why'd he have to say that? I was just starting to like him ... a little.* She responded, "They worked fine. I just thought I'd be more comfortable in sneakers."

He gave her a knowing smile and said, "Right, but next time we go to town, maybe we should get you some boots. They would be easier to clean than your pretty sandals and sneakers."

Fuming inside, she tromped behind him to check the fences. After a few minutes, she forgot about being mad, because it was so beautiful in the mountains. It wasn't Florida, but she loved it.

Her short time in Colorado had certainly been full of surprises. She was surprised the air was so clean and clear and was surprised that after her uncle gave her a jacket to wear, she liked the coolness. She found the mountains to be spectacular and discovered getting up early in the morning could be a good thing. But most of all, she was surprised she liked a certain horse, and loved touching her muzzle. She had to admit maybe Colorado had more good things to offer than she'd expected.

CHAPTER 4
Getting to Know Uncle Mark and Shasta

MARK HUBBARD PROVED to be a man of few words, except when he saw something along the trail that might interest his niece. As they walked, they checked the fences, and when they found a spot where they could see the beautiful, weather-ravaged top of Longs Peak, he stopped and pulled out a thermos of hot chocolate.

At this point, Julie was so thirsty she didn't even complain when she and her uncle had to share the same cup. She just looked up at him and smiled.

He commented, "You know, you should smile more often, Julie. You remind me of your mom when you do."

She blushed and looked the other way. Since she'd been in Colorado, she hadn't been overwhelmed with thoughts of her parents, like she had been in Florida. He had just reminded her that her mom was gone forever, and she felt guilty. Guilty because she'd let her new life in Colorado overshadow thinking about her parents.

Living at the Estes Park Wilderness Outfitters taught her a lot of things, including some things she'd rather not know. She now knew how to muck out a stall, stack hay, and turn horses out in the pasture. She did learn one interesting fact, though, but she didn't know when she'd be able to slip it into a conversation with her friends. Someone had mentioned that mules were sterile, so you could only get a baby mule by mating a horse with a donkey. She'd been wondering why they kept those little donkeys around, because they had plenty of mules they could breed. Maybe her friends in Florida would find that interesting—but probably not! Speaking of her Florida friends, they didn't call. For a while she called them to see how everyone was, but they never called her first, so she guessed they were too busy with their own lives.

Julie had been going to school in Estes Park for a couple of months now, but because she lived on the outskirts of town, she felt she could never ask kids to come over and visit. That was okay, though, because she still had Shasta and Brutus. She thought, *It's pretty lame when my best friends are a horse and a dog. A new low for me.*

When she thought about her Uncle Mark, she had to admit he'd been pretty good to her. Even though he wasn't a Christian, he took the time to drive her to church on Sunday. Maybe one day he'd stay for a service. She'd have to pray about that.

***

One evening that fall, Julie and Uncle Mark were sitting in the living room reading. She had a *Girls Life* magazine, and he was thumbing through the latest *Estes Park Gazette*. Looking around the room, she thought it was cozy with the fire going. She never remembered her parents sitting around in the evening with her … or even reading. They were always going out somewhere. In fact, the two of them had been flying down to Mexico for a week when they were killed. She had always stayed with her Aunt Fran when they traveled, which wasn't too bad, because her aunt let her stay up late and spend the night with her friends whenever she wanted. Fat chance Uncle Mark would let her do anything like that. He was always paraphrasing the old saying, "Early to bed, early to rise, makes Julie healthy, wealthy, and wise." Sometimes he could be so old-fashioned. But she smiled at the thought, and in a strange way it made her feel he cared for her. He always knew where she was and would've been mad if he didn't.

Julie broke the silence, "Uncle Mark, were you ever married?"
He looked up from his reading and stared at her. "Where did
that question come from?"

"I was just wondering, because you have the perfect place for a
family, and you seem to get along with me okay."

"That question is kind of personal, but I'll answer it. Yes, I was
married—a long time ago."

"Did you ever want kids?"

He squirmed in his chair before he answered. "Actually, I had
a son."

She was curious. "Where is he now?"

"He died with his mom in a car crash." He added, "If you don't
mind, I'd rather not talk about this right now." He looked at his
watch and started to get out of his chair. "I think it's about time for
us to hit the sack anyway. You have school tomorrow, and I have a
busy day planned."

Julie objected. "Uncle Mark, I *don't* have school tomorrow
because we're on Christmas break. In fact, Christmas is only two
days away."

He apologized. "Sorry, kid, but I'm not used to keeping track of
those kinds of things. I've lived alone a long time."

***

Julie spent most of her Christmas vacation taking care of Shasta.
The mare was very big now and looked uncomfortable. Julie kept her
stall clean and brushed her several times a day, because she didn't
know when she would have her baby. Julie didn't want the mare to
deliver her foal in dirty or soiled straw, so she kept it clean and fresh.

Christmas Eve came, and Julie and her uncle exchanged presents.
She'd found him a nice pair of wool socks and a warm scarf, which
surprised him because he hadn't taken her into town to shop. His
gift to her was the heavy shearling coat she'd seen in a catalog and
an Amazon gift card so she could choose something else she liked.

The evening was restful, and they quietly listened to Christmas
carols on the radio. The beautiful songs made Julie think about the

first Christmas. "Uncle Mark, I love this time of year because we get to celebrate our Savior's birth. It was probably on a night like this he was born. I can't imagine how Mary rode all those miles to Bethlehem on a donkey and then had her baby in a stable, especially since she had to use a manger of hay for a crib."

Uncle Mark quietly commented, "I used to know all those stories."

Julie responded, "Uncle Mark, they *aren't* just stories. They really happened. God's son came to earth as a tiny baby."

He said no more.

CHAPTER 5
Christmas Day and a Foal is Born

BEFORE THEY WENT up to bed, Julie said, "I know it's past midnight, but I'm going to check on Shasta one more time and wish her a Merry Christmas, because the vet said she's due to have her foal anytime." She put on her new coat and trudged out into the frosty night to Barn 2.

When she peeked at Shasta over the stall door, she could see the mare pacing nervously around her stall, and she looked like she was getting ready to lie down. "What's the matter, girl? Are you okay?" The reply was a soft nicker.

Suddenly, it occurred to Julie the mare was about to have her baby. She turned immediately and ran back to the lodge. She burst in the front door and called out, "Uncle Mark, I think Shasta is ready to have her foal. You need to come now!" Then she ran back to the barn.

Minutes later he appeared with a flashlight so they could see exactly what was going on with the mare. When he shined the light in the stall, he could see she was now lying down, struggling to give birth. They were amazed when they saw the foal's front legs, then its head, and finally with one grunt, its whole body appeared. Mark bent over to see. "It's a boy—a little colt!"

Julie was thrilled as she glanced over at her uncle. "She did it!"

Then she knelt beside Shasta and patted her neck. "You are such a good girl. And you brought this beautiful colt into the world on Christmas Day. How special. We should name him Christmas, but that's too hard to say if we have to call him in from the pasture, but we'll think of a good name."

Uncle Mark agreed to attend church with Julie that day, which was a wonderful gift and an answer to her prayers. She was disappointed he looked uncomfortable during the service, though she felt sure God had been a part of his life at some point. This was a step in the right direction.

After church, Mark and Julie returned to the barn to check on mother and son. She was surprised to see the foal already up and nursing, but her uncle wasn't surprised and just smiled. "Isn't nature wonderful? Horses are not like humans. We're totally helpless at birth."

The days became routine for Julie. She would get up early, check on Shasta and her little one, feed the horses, go to school, check on Shasta again, do her homework, and then check on the horses yet again. Somehow this mare and her foal had become the central focus of her life.

One evening, after they'd checked on their favorite horses, Mark asked, "Aren't you ever going to name that foal? He's three weeks old and can't be called 'the foal' forever."

Julie turned to him in surprise. "Uncle Mark, he's not mine to name. He's yours."

Her uncle laughed and responded, "No one around here would ever think that. You're doting on him every free second you have."

"I just like doing it. But he's still *your* horse."

Mark responded, "I seem to remember you have a birthday coming up the end of January."

"What difference does that make?" Then it dawned on her what he might mean. "You've got to be kidding me. You mean you might be giving me Shasta's foal for my birthday?"

"Why not? It keeps me from having to buy you a present. I never know what to give someone, so it seems like giving him to you solves my problem."

Julie ran into his arms and hugged his neck. "Oh, thank you, thank you, Uncle Mark. No one has ever given me such a special present."

He carefully peeled her off him and grinned. "Now let's not go overboard with the hugs and kisses. I'm not used to that kind of stuff."

She smiled. "*Now* I can give him a name. I'll think about it tonight, because it has to be a really special one." Then she ran to her room to decide what she'd call the colt.

At breakfast the next day she told her uncle she'd decided on a name. "Though it would be nice to name him Christmas, because he was born on Christmas Day, that could be a problem. I was trying to think of a snazzy but easy name and came up with Black Jazz. We could register him as Black Jazz, but I could always call him Jazz or Jazzy, whichever is easier to say. What do you think?"

Mark answered, "Well, he's definitely black, so, yes, that would be a good name. He's your horse, so you can name him whatever you choose."

CHAPTER 6
Do You Blame God?

SPRING ARRIVED, AND with spring came freedom, especially freedom for the horses to spend more time outside. Julie had treasured watching Jazz experience his first snow but was especially enthralled with seeing his reaction to wildflowers and butterflies. Other horses on the ranch had new foals, but Julie loved her little guy best. He loved to run and play with the others then run and hide behind his mom when they came after him.

***

Jazz was now weaned and seemed to spend more time with Rufus, Julie's other animal friend. They romped and rolled as much as they could. It was crazy seeing the bond between the young foal and a pup, who now had almost grown into his big feet. They were inseparable.

Aunt Fran and Uncle Fred seldom called, but when they did Julie did her best to keep the conversation short. She was happy in Colorado and was afraid they might want her to come back and live with them in Florida. She suspected they thought of her only when the attorneys called, updating them on the status of the class action suit filed in her parent's accident. She didn't want to leave her new home. It surprised Julie she'd come to love Uncle Mark, even though he was strict with her and insisted she work on the ranch. She never doubted he loved and wanted to protect her. *Boy*, she thought, *is this what growing up is—changing your value system, because you realize people who care for you can be tough because they love you?*

One day Julie asked her uncle, "I know you occasionally attend church with me, but I wonder why you seem uncomfortable there. I know it's not the people, because they're all your friends."

He squirmed like he always did when she asked him something personal, and then he asked, "Have you ever blamed God for your parents' death?"

Julie responded immediately. "No, of course not. They flew on a plane that turned out to be unsafe and crashed. God had nothing to do with it."

Her uncle continued with another question. "Couldn't he have stopped it from crashing?"

Julie answered. "God doesn't manage everything, even though he could. There are consequences to airlines if they don't keep their planes safe. Sometimes accidents happen, and people are caught up in those consequences."

Mark was quiet, and because she was uncomfortable with his silence, she continued. "For instance, I blame my parents for leaving me, not the airline." She was shocked, because she hadn't meant to say that. She'd never admitted *that* to anyone. What a terrible thing to say— that she blamed her parents.

Mark didn't say anything but let her talk. "I mean, if they hadn't gone on that trip …"

Mark asked her, "So you are telling me you haven't forgiven them for leaving you?"

Julie squirmed uncomfortably. "Uncle Mark, you're putting words in my mouth."

He didn't let her go. "Julie, that's exactly what I heard."

She had tears in her eyes. "It wouldn't be right to blame them *or* God."

He decided to drop the subject but explained his own reasons for blaming God. "My family left me too. Not because they were in an accident … at least not initially. My wife was very unhappy living here on the ranch, because it was so far away from the city. She'd finally had enough, took my son, and left. It was only later they were killed in a traffic accident. It's been easier to blame my wife and God than to blame myself, but deep down I know I had a big part in their leaving."

Julie apologized. "I'm so sorry I brought up those memories."

"It's okay, but I have to ask you another question. How did you get over the pain and the blame?"

She answered thoughtfully. "Well, evidently I *haven't* gotten over the blame, but I'm working on it. God's helping me forgive my folks, but it seems to be a process. I keep giving my hurt feelings to him, and he keeps handing them back to me, and will until I've truly forgiven them. It's amazing how it gets easier each time, and it helps to try to look at the positive things that have happened since they died. I must admit going to church and living with you have been blessings to me. If they hadn't died, I would've continued my life as it was, which meant I would be left alone a lot and felt unloved. And I wouldn't have met you and come to love horses, especially Shasta and Jazz. God did that for me." She looked over at him. "Maybe in some way I've been a blessing to you, too."

When Mark glanced her way, she saw tears in his eyes. "That's probably true, because, Jules, in less than a year I've come to love you like I would a daughter— something I swore I'd never do again. I thought giving your heart to someone left you vulnerable and unprotected—inviting them to stomp on it and hurt you. I no longer have that fear."

Julie got up and put her arms around him, but he laughed and pushed her away. "You've got to quit that hugging stuff; it makes me cry." She hugged him anyway, and he hugged her back.

CHAPTER 7
The Picnic

THE SUMMER MEANT no school, but it also meant a lot more work. Estes Park Wilderness Outfitters was extremely busy, which left less time for Shasta and Jazz. Julie thought she'd resent the long hours, but she loved them. She was meeting new people all the time, learning more about horses and the business, and felt like she was becoming an invaluable part of a team. That was something she'd never felt in Florida, and she probably never would've had that feeling. It seemed she seldom thought of Florida anymore, because there was so much to think about and do in Colorado.

One afternoon, Uncle Mark asked her if she'd like to go on a picnic the next day. She knew they were busy at work, but he insisted they take a little time off. He wanted to show her some of the trails where his crew took their riders and suggested she ride Shasta because she needed exercise. The mare hadn't been ridden since before Jazz was born, so he knew she'd enjoy getting out. Jazz was young and would follow them.

The Outfitters' cook packed them a wonderful picnic basket for the outing. When they started out, Jazz was a little skittish about being away from the safety of the ranch. Because he was still little, he wanted to be near his mom. Julie kept looking back to make sure he was following them. The colt was inquisitive and looked around, and shied at every strange noise or movement. His world had only been the ranch, so the wide-open spaces both excited and frightened him.

They followed rocky, winding trails, and even crossed a few streams, which was a shock to the young foal. If he'd been tethered to his mom, she would've had to drag him across the streams, because the water was ice cold and sometimes flowed fast. At the water crossings, he'd stop dead in his tracks, until he saw he was being left behind, and then he'd plunge across to catch up.

When they stopped beside a stream that afternoon, Julie scooped up a cup of ice-cold water to take a drink. Mark quickly grabbed her cup and poured out the water. "Jules, that water looks cold and refreshing, but you can't see all the bacteria in it. It doesn't matter that it looks clear and clean; I've followed streams upstream many times and found dead animals lying in them, not to mention what beaver and other animals may have done in the water. I wouldn't take a chance and drink it, because you may get really sick and ruin, not just your day, but your whole week."

She looked at him in surprise. "But I've always heard how wonderful and clean water was in cool mountain streams and how good it tastes."

He looked at her and asked, "Think about what I said. Fish alone dirty water. Have you ever had a fishbowl?"

"Well, yes."

"Why did you have to clean it?"

She replied when she finally understood. "Oh yeah, I remember now. It looked disgusting. You couldn't have paid me to drink it."

He smiled and handed her a canteen. "This water is much better for you, even if it isn't as cold as you'd like."

Uncle Mark pulled their lunches out of his saddlebag while Julie spread a colorful checkered cloth on a large rock nearby. Once they were settled, he passed her some fried chicken and scooped potato salad onto her plate. She took a few bites then leaned back, tilting her face up to the sun. "It's only sixty degrees outside, but the sun feels great up here. It feels almost as warm as the beach."

Her uncle commented, "People in the mountains often forget to use sunscreen because they don't realize a person gets sunburned quicker at higher altitudes." He added, "Thanks for reminding me," then he passed her his sunscreen.

Julie started to argue with him about burning quicker in the mountains, but he stopped her. "Direct UV-B levels in Vail are the same as those in Orlando, which is actually 775 miles closer to the equator. The higher the altitude, the more intense the UV-B light exposure, which can damage unprotected skin. And, don't forget, the atmosphere is thinner up here in the mountains, so it gives you less protection from the sun."

Julie was amazed. "Uncle Mark, you sound like a doctor."

He laughed. "You don't think all I've done with my life is raise pack animals, do you?"

"What *did* you do that made you so smart?"

"Well, I got a bachelor of science degree in atmospheric sciences because I wanted to be a meteorologist, which by the way, qualifies you to be a weatherman."

Julie was interested. "So you were a weather broadcaster on television?"

"I'm afraid not. I worked behind the scenes. Actually, I worked for NOAA, which is the National Oceanic and Atmospheric Administration."

"What's that, and what do they do?"

"It's an American scientific agency within the US Department of Commerce. Its focus is mainly oceanic and atmospheric conditions. NOAA warns the public of dangerous weather; you know, like hurricanes. I worked in a unit conducting research to help us understand and take care of the environment."

Julie nodded her head. "*Now* I understand why you know so much about the atmosphere and UV light. Why don't you work at NOAA anymore?"

Her uncle laughed. "My, my, aren't you full of questions today. The simple answer is, I've always been fond of horses and the mountains, so when I retired, I moved here, bought this outfitter business, and I love it."

Softly, Julie said, "I'm glad you did."

Once she packed away the remaining food and trash, she took a brush out of her saddlebag and approached Jazz. "Come here, sweetheart. Let's put this rope around your neck for a minute. I want you to stand still while I brush you."

He nickered and moved toward her, because he recognized the brush and loved it when she groomed him. He knew she always scratched and rubbed the places he couldn't reach.

Fifteen minutes later Uncle Mark commented, "You're going to rub the hair right off that colt. He's already shiny as black glass. Once you finish, let's mount up. If we hurry, we can probably make it to Odessa Lake before we have to turn around and head for home."

As they rode along, Julie commented, "Uncle Mark, this has been a wonderful day. I didn't realize how much I needed this break, so thank you."

"My pleasure, Jules."

CHAPTER 8
Learning More about Friesian Horses

ONE EVENING AFTER dinner, Mark asked, "Julie, remember I told you someday I'd tell you more about the history of the Friesian breed. I figure since you own one now, you'd be interested."

"Yes, I remember. I'd forgotten all about it."

"Go cut us a piece of that cake you made this afternoon, and I'll tell you all about them."

When she returned with the cake and sat down, Mark began the history lesson. "As you know, my friend gave me Shasta, so naturally I looked into her background. The Friesian horse is a breed from Friesland, which is a province of the Netherlands. Friesians were originally bred as draft horses, but they turned out to be graceful and nimble for their size. Later, the horse developed into a fine-boned nobleman's steed. During the Middle Ages, they were greatly valued by knights who wore full armor, because Friesians were strong and larger than many other horse breeds of that time."

He winked at her and asked, "Had enough?" She shook her head no so he continued. "The Friesian's average height is about 15.3 hands, but its height may vary from 14.2 to 17 hands tall at the withers, which is really tall." He stopped a minute and asked, "You remember me telling you one hand equals 4 inches, don't you?" She

nodded yes. "Jazzy will get big, but probably not 17 hands tall."
He continued. "If you've watched Shasta, you know Friesians have a spectacular trot, which is both fast and high-stepping. You also know they are very sweet-natured horses and are easy to train, because by nature they want to please."

He took a sip of his coffee then cleared his throat. "By looking at Shasta and Jazz, you can see the breed has excellent conformation. I'm also sure you've noticed their long, elegant, arched necks and fine-boned heads, which is *very* different from some of the mulish pack animals I have here. Their shoulders are powerful, and their bodies are muscular and compact. Friesians also have impressive hair, which I'm sure you've noticed as well."

Julie commented, "I *have* noticed her long mane and tail and the long hair that covers their lower legs and hooves."

"The hair on their fetlocks is, believe it or not, called feathers. A lot of the draft horses, like the Clydesdales—you know, the Budweiser Beer horses I told you about—have feathers as well."

"Yes, Jazz and Shasta both have those feathers."

He teased her. "Do you want to hear more, or is it past your bedtime?"

"Of course I want to hear more. Besides, it's only seven-thirty."

He recounted more of what he'd learned. "Since the Friesians have a heavy, muscular physique, they aren't very good at sports like racing, but they make wonderful dressage horses because of their flashy action."

"Yes, I've seen that action in Shasta, and even in Jazzy, even though he's still young."

"The gait you see is very natural to the breed, because it was bred into them through the years. Like I was saying, the Friesian is used mainly for dressage, but it's also popular as a carriage horse. One reason it makes a great carriage horse is it's easy to match teams of Friesians because they're usually all black, and their high-stepping action makes them very impressive."

Julie was curious. "Can they be used for jumping?"

"Not really, but they're great for general riding, for showing, driving, and they also make good circus horses."

Julie had another question. "How long do their manes and tails get? Shasta's mane is about two feet long."

He explained. "I've seen pictures of Friesian horses whose manes *and* tails drag the ground. And yes, I said *both* their manes and their tails drag the ground. Hard to imagine, isn't it?"

"Really?" She was amazed.

"Yup. Next time you're online, look up photographs of Friesian horses, and you'll see for yourself. Sometimes their manes and tails are not straight, but very wavy. In fact, owners of these horses often braid or tie up their horse's manes and tails so they don't step on them, getting them dirty and knotted. Of course, they're brushed out when they show them because flowing manes and tails are sought-after traits in this breed. I don't think you have to worry about Shasta, though. She's probably grown all the mane she's going to grow."

"Uncle Mark, thank you for telling me about Friesians. I never would've guessed they had such a colorful history. When I go upstairs, I'm going to Google pictures of them, so I can see their super long manes and tails."

After she took their plates to the sink and started upstairs, she heard her uncle say, "Sweet dreams, Jules."

CHAPTER 9
Aunt Fran Wants Julie Back

AUTUMN CAME AND turned the aspen leaves to a beautiful yellow gold. People wanting to ride and camp in the Rockies loved to see and ride among the leaves in the fall. The Outfitters was a very busy place this time of year, but Mark knew Julie was his responsibility, so he usually stayed home and sent others out with the overnight campers. His niece had been there almost a year now, and he didn't know how he'd ever lived without her. She was curious, helpful, funny, smart, and most of all, loving. He complained every time she reached up to give him a big hug or kiss him, but she knew he loved it. He hadn't had a family in a long, long time, and it felt especially right taking care of his sister's child.

Mark knew Julie got calls from Florida, but he truly believed she now loved it here, and he didn't know what he'd do if she decided to leave. Fortunately, he'd had the foresight to get guardianship papers drawn up so he'd have the legal right to raise her in Colorado. He wondered what would happen once her parents' class action suit was settled. Would there be a battle for custody? He hoped not. Would Julie be tempted to return to the warm sands of Florida? He didn't even want to think about it.

Christmas vacation was upon them again. This time he

remembered, and a few days before Christmas, Julie approached him and asked, "Would it be okay if we celebrate Jazz's first birthday? Maybe we could give him carrots, apples, oatmeal-honey granola bars, and sing "Happy Birthday" to him? Oh! and Starlight mints. I gave him a few once, and he loved them."

Her uncle laughed. "You're crazy, Jules. I've never, *ever* celebrated a horse's birthday, nor even thought about doing so."

Julie chirped, "There's always a first time, Uncle Mark, and besides, it will be Christmas, so we can treat Jazz and Shasta to a little holiday spirit. I'm sure Brutus would come to the party."

"Okay, okay, I'll come, but you'll have to arrange it." And she did.

***

Winter melted into spring, and spring blossomed into summer. School was out, and Estes Park Wilderness Outfitters was humming. Foals had been born, summer crews had been hired, and the phone was ringing off the hook, wanting to buy or lease pack animals, or to take treks into the wilderness. The days flew by; then Mark received a call from his sister, Fran. His sister and Julie's aunt from Florida.

"Hi there, brother. It's been a long time. I've talked with Julie, but not with you since you agreed to keep her for a while. I have some exciting news! The case settled, and there will be a payout next month. I think she'll be pleased with her share of the settlement."

Mark felt a chill run down his spine, but he responded with courtesy. "That's nice, Fran. If there's anything for Julie to sign, just send it to us, and I'll get her to sign it and send it back. I think you know my address."

Fran sounded alarmed. "But, Mark, Julie must come home now. She was raised in Florida and belongs here. We thank you for all you've done for her, but she needs to come back to her *real* home. We all knew her staying with you was only temporary."

"Fran, Julie isn't here right now, but I'll have her call you when she gets in."

"Well, okay." Fran sounded disappointed she couldn't speak with

Julie because she was excited about the news. "We can hardly wait to tell her she'll finally be coming home to Florida, so be sure and tell her to call us as soon as possible."

Mark was numb when he hung up the phone.

A few minutes later Julie came into the house, wiping her feet at the door. "It's raining, Uncle Mark." She wasn't sure he was home because the house was so quiet. "Uncle Mark, where are you?" She found him sitting at the kitchen table, deep in thought.

She was confused. "What's going on? Why didn't you answer me?" He turned to her. She noticed he had tears in his eyes. Now she was alarmed. "What's happening? What's wrong?

He simply motioned for her to sit down, which scared her even more. "Your aunt called a few minutes ago, and she wants you to call her back right away."

Julie shrugged her shoulders. "She calls every once in a while, so what's the hurry? Is there a problem?"

He answered without emotion. "She wants you to move back to Florida, because your case settled."

His words were met with a belligerent snort. "*This* is my home now. I don't want to go back. She shoved me out when it wasn't convenient to take care of me, and now I have you. You *are* my legal guardian, aren't you?" He nodded yes.

"Then what's the problem?"

Mark reached over and pulled her onto his lap. "Jules, life isn't always logical or simple. Your aunt may try to get you back through the court system. You're only thirteen now, and the judge may think it would be in your best interest to be with a female relative, not a grumpy old uncle with no wife who lives on a ranch in the middle of nowhere."

Julie protested. "But I love this grumpy old, single uncle." Her hand flew to her mouth. Though she'd known she loved him for a long time, she'd never actually told him. Would this sudden admission shock him?

Instead, he cuddled her closer. "I love you too, Jules. Let's not worry about this mess for a while. In fact, give your aunt a call, then let's go play hooky. I'm not leading any rides today, so it'd be a great time to explore another lake. How about it?"

She quickly nodded. "Sounds wonderful to me," but then she whined, "Do I have to call her first?"

"Yup, that's the deal. Just like when you work outside with me, we get the unpleasant jobs done before we play."

Julie looked sad when she returned from the other room. "Aunt Fran and Uncle Fred have bought tickets to Denver and will be here tomorrow to see me. They want to take me home with them."

Her uncle asked, "What do *you* want to do, Julie? You know I won't stand in your way if you want to go."

She ran to her room and threw herself on her bed, crying out, "Why? Why yank me away from someone who loves me and from Jazz? He's here and I want to stay with him!" She sobbed into her pillow until she could cry no more.

Uncle Mark had followed her upstairs and stood outside her door, listening. He choked back tears as he heard her sobs. He loved Julie and didn't want her to be snatched away any more than she wanted to go. He stayed until he sensed she'd cried herself to sleep and then tiptoed to his room to think. Surely there had to be a way to keep her here. She loved Colorado, the horses, and him. That was a shock. She had actually said she loved him.

Mark had grown up with Fran, and her selfish, bossy personality was the biggest reason he'd left home and never gone back. She'd *always* been hard to deal with if she didn't get her way, and she wanted her way now.

CHAPTER 10
Aunt Fran Wants Julie Back

THOUGH THE NEXT day was sunny and bright, the mood around the lodge was not. Julie barely touched her breakfast and told her uncle she was going out to see Shasta and Jazz. He could hear the pain in her voice.

Fran and Fred were not due in until about two o'clock that afternoon, but he knew he wouldn't get much work done this morning thinking about the showdown ahead. He absolutely *knew* he wasn't going to give her up without a fight.

The shuttle dropping off people coming from the Denver airport was a little late, adding to Mark's stress. When it arrived, he greeted those who had reservations with his outfit and then turned to Fran and Fred. Her clothes were wrinkled, and she was tired, but she looked around, eagerly trying to spot her precious niece—the one she had quickly packed off to him almost two years ago.

She looked at Mark and demanded, "Where's Julie? I expected her to be here waiting, because it's been so long since she's seen me."

Mark thought, *It's so like Fran to expect Julie to be excited about seeing her. My sister still thinks the world revolves around her, so I wonder if she's even thought Julie might want to stay here and not go back to Florida. Of course not.*

Fran demanded again, "Well, where is she? I came all this way to see her."

Mark answered, "I suppose she might be in the barn with her horse."

Fran's eyes opened wide. "She has a horse? How can she take a horse back to Florida? What on earth is she doing with a horse?"

Mark answered quietly. "It was a birthday present from me."

Her eyes narrowed, and she responded tartly, "Mark, you *know* she can't have a horse in Florida."

He responded, "I'm leaving it up to you to tell her that. She loves that colt."

Fran moved toward him with barely concealed hate in her eyes and screamed, spit flying from her lips. "So you're trying to bribe her to stay here?"

Mark responded calmly. "I already told you the colt was a birthday present, Fran, not a bribe."

"Harrumph," she snorted. "So you say." She turned to her husband. "Fred, let's go inside and wait until Julie gets here."

When they stomped loudly up the steps, Mark turned and headed for the barn. He was surprised Shasta and Jazz were nowhere to be found. He called for Julie but got no answer. Then he looked in the pasture and didn't find his niece, the horses, or the dog. He thought, *I hope she hasn't done anything stupid.* Ten minutes later he knew she had.

He reluctantly returned to the lodge. "I guess Julie's out with the horses. I couldn't find her."

Fran turned to her husband. "See, I told you he was going to try to interfere with us taking her back." She whirled around and spoke between clinched teeth. "You *know*, I never liked you when we were growing up, because you were sneaky, and this proves it. You'd *better* get some people together and find her, because we have a plane to catch this evening." She added menacingly, "I don't want to have to call the authorities to get her back."

Mark could hardly believe what he was hearing, and he responded, "I believe I'm her guardian, not you, and I have the court documents to prove it."

Fran shut her mouth in surprise. Then between clinched teeth she said, "We'll see about that."

Mark gathered up all available hands on the ranch and sent them out to find Julie and the horses. They searched for hours with no success. Mark was worried but realized the reason Julie had left was because she didn't want to go back to Florida. That meant she really liked it here and wanted to stay. By ten that evening he was *very* concerned, and it didn't help that Fran was continually accusing him of sending her away.

He finally turned to her in disgust. "Do you *really* think I want Julie out in the woods alone this time of night? I'm worried too, and I'm blaming this on *you* because she cried herself to sleep last night knowing you wanted to take her back to Florida."

Fran was speechless but finally sputtered, "I know what's best for her. What can you give her here besides horses and manure?"

Mark answered levelly. "How about compassion for animals and people, love, stability, and I teach her responsibility. Fran, I'm not some uneducated boob who would *ever* neglect her education, because I know how important it is." He paused. "Do you know anything about me, Fran? What I've done with my life since I left home? And, if you thought I was such a poor placement choice, why did you send her here in the first place? That might be seen as child endangerment or neglect in a court of law."

CHAPTER 11
Uncle Mark Persuades Aunt to Leave Without Julie

FUMING, SHE AND Fred turned and marched to their rooms.

The next morning, Julie still had not returned. Mark thought to himself, *Jules, this isn't the way to solve our problem, but I thank God you are resourceful and pray you remember the survival skills I taught you.* Though he hadn't prayed for a very long time, he bowed his head. *God, I know you are there, because you were with me once. It's really my fault, because I chose to leave you when my family split up, and they were later killed. My plea is that Julie is found unharmed, because I know you love her, and so do I. If she's okay and wants to go back to Florida, I'll let her go. But if it's your will she stays here in Colorado with me, I need your help.* Mark choked back a sob. *I know you can move mountains. Holy Spirit, give me either the ability to accept an outcome I don't like, or put words in my mouth that will keep her here, safe with me. Amen.*

Julie returned late the next day, tired and hungry. When Mark saw her, he rushed to her with arms open wide and gave her a big hug. "Thank God you're okay!" But then he pushed her back, grabbed her shoulders, and scolded her. "Don't you *ever* do that again. Do you hear me? *Never!*"

Her first words to him were, "The horses needed oats." Then she smiled weakly and said, "Aunt Fran and Uncle Fred are still here, aren't they?"

Her uncle nodded yes.

Once the horses were fed and in their stalls, they walked to the house, with Mark's arm slung protectively over her shoulders.

Fran and Fred were waiting for them on the porch. Immediately Fran demanded, "What do you have to say for yourself, young lady? We missed our flight."

Julie bravely looked up at them. "I left because I love it here and want to stay."

"Preposterous! You belong with us in Florida."

Julie asked, "Why? Why do you want me now?"

Her aunt answered, "Well, you can't get your insurance settlement until you come back to Florida and sign it, and that's important."

"Why would that make a difference, Aunt Fran? I have everything I need here with Uncle Mark."

Without thinking, her aunt answered, "Well, when you come back, we can get a bigger and nicer house, and you can have your friends over to celebrate. You can buy lots of new clothes, and when you're old enough to drive, you can buy a new car. Don't you want that?"

Julie would have rolled her eyes, but she knew it would only make her aunt mad. "I already told you I love it here, and I have Jazz to think about."

Fran had an answer ready. "Sweetheart, you can have someone haul your horse to Florida and find a stable to take care of him."

"You don't understand. This is Jazz's home, and his mother is here as well. I want to take care of them myself."

Fran wrinkled her nose. "You actually *like* taking care of horses?"

"Yes, I do."

Uncle Mark stepped forward and looked directly at Fran. "You didn't even ask Julie how she was. Weren't you even a little bit concerned she may have been hurt? She's been gone more than a day—overnight, in fact."

Fran answered coolly, "I can see she's okay, so I didn't need to ask her."

Mark ignored her response and continued. "It's clear Julie wants to stay in Colorado. I'm her legal guardian, so until a court changes my status, you are to go back to Florida and leave her alone."

He heard a snort of disagreement from Fran, but he continued. "A child custody dispute would have to be settled here in Larimer County, and months may pass before you get an attorney, sit for depositions, and a hearing is set. Are you two ready to fly back and forth between here and Florida to attend those proceedings? Please remember what I told you earlier. Several things will be considered, and ultimately the court will determine what is in Julie's best interest. She's now thirteen years old, so her preference *will* be considered in their determination. She's happy, healthy, and has made friends here."

Without taking a breath he continued. "Julie has a church home in Estes Park as well—one she loves and attends regularly. I understand in Florida Julie rarely went to church—and then only with friends, not with you and Fred. I've grown to love my niece, and I've taken care of her for almost two years, *without* being paid. As I mentioned before, you let her come here without checking out my background first. As far as you knew, I could have been a child molester. You only knew I was her uncle and having me take care of her was convenient and cheaper for you. You wanted to warehouse her here until her money came in."

Fran was mad, and she interrupted. "That's not fair! We had no money to keep her back then."

Mark laughed. "And now? You have more money now?"

"When Julie's settlement is paid out, we'll have plenty of money to take care of her, because we'll be her guardians."

"And you love her?"

"Of course we love her."

Mark smiled. "And how often did you speak with her when she was here or send a little money to help her out? Remember, I can get telephone records not only listing the number of calls, but the number of minutes you talked."

Fran replied defensively, "We *did* have contact with her though. Calling costs money as well."

Mark pressed on. "I'm sure you have long-distance minutes on your cell phones. It's not like the old days when you would have been billed for those minutes each month. And how about Christmas presents?"

"We sent a card with some money in it."

He asked, "How much money, Fran? And remember, we're going to ask Julie—under oath—if we must go to court."

Fran sounded defensive. "Five dollars, but it's not about the money. We just didn't have it to give."

Mark put up his hand and stopped her. "May I ask how you are getting back to Florida and return for the court dates, if you have no money?" He continued. "You will lose your case against me, because it's become quite evident you are counting on Julie's money so you can live better in the future. I am her blood relative as well; she has a two-year history with me, and she's happy. It appears you've wasted the little money you say you have, by traveling clear out here to pick her up. I really don't know how you'll be able to afford the travel required and an attorney, as well as the court fees. You might as well cut your losses, Fran, and give up."

Julie could hardly believe what she was hearing. Mark was defending her, and she might be able to stay in Colorado. She prayed, *Dear God, you know the desire of my heart is to stay here with my family. Uncle Mark, Shasta, Jazzy, and Brutus are now my family. But I also know, if I must go back to Florida, you'll always be with me and be my best friend, so I'll be okay. Amen.*

Fran snarled at her brother. "How dare you say it's all about the money. I've missed Julie."

Mark looked over at his niece, who was looking at him so hopefully. He looked back at his sister. "I have a proposition, Fran. If you continue to pursue this, you will lose, which means you will have wasted what money you've already put out. I will pay you $2,000 to cover your expenses for the month she was with you after her parents died, and the airfare you paid to get her out here. But you must promise to let go of the notion you are going to drag Julie back to Florida, whether she likes it or not."

Fran snorted in disgust. "We've put out more money than that. We also bought round-trip tickets out here, as well as a one-way ticket back for Julie. That alone cost us almost $2,000."

Mark countered. "Okay, I'll make it an even $6,000, if you sign an agreement to never try to take her away from me again."

Fred noticed his wife look at Mark and his offer with disdain, so he tried to reason with her. "Honey, take the money, and let's go home. It was a bad idea anyway."

She sputtered as she struggled to swallow her pride and then responded to the offer. "We'll take it, but we want the money *now*."

Mark smiled. "Agreed," he said and went to get his checkbook. When he returned, he noticed tears in Fran's eyes when she looked at Julie. He hoped it was because she loved her niece and would miss her, but more likely she was thinking about the gold mine she'd lost forever. His suspicions were confirmed when after he handed her the check and she signed the agreement, she, with Fred following her, turned and walked out the door without saying a word. He thought, *So much for a loving family.*

CHAPTER 12
Julie Explains her Flight from Aunt

WHEN THEY WERE gone, Julie was relieved. "Whew, Uncle Mark, I was afraid I was going to have to go back to Florida with them, but you talked them into letting me stay. Thank you for speaking up for me."

"You're welcome, but I still have something to say to you, young lady." His voice became louder, and he started shaking. "Don't you *ever* go into the woods like that again. You were gone more than twenty-four hours, and I was worried sick. You could have been attacked by a bear or a mountain lion!" He tried to calm down. "Julie, I believe you owe me an apology and a promise."

She looked at him, apologized, and promised to never run off again.

He had expected her to tear up and cry because he was yelling at her, but instead she gave him a big smile. Confused, he asked, "Why are you smiling? I'm furious with you."

The smile never left her face. "I'm smiling because you love me and want me to stay with you. You wouldn't have gotten so mad if you didn't care."

With that she ran into his arms and gave him all the hugs

and kisses he could stand. He tried to push her away, but he was laughing, so she knew he loved it.

He made a face and laughed. "Jules, you may think I'm pushing you away because I don't like the kisses, but it's because you need a shower. Get your bottom upstairs and get cleaned up." When she left, he thought, *She doesn't really smell bad, but knowing her, she's probably tired and has been dreaming about a hot shower and how good it would feel to be clean again.* He sat down in his chair and was surprised at how good it felt to have his Jules home where she belonged.

***

After breakfast the next morning, Mark said, "Feed the horses and turn them out in their paddocks; then come sit down with me. I want to debrief you on what happened the day you were having your *adventure*."

While Julie was out doing her chores, he made them some hot chocolate. When she returned, he handed her a cup and then motioned for her to sit down on the couch next to him. "Okay, two days ago you went to see the horses and then suddenly decided to take them into the woods. Is that right?"

"Uncle Mark, it really wasn't like that. I went to check on them and started crying again. I was still in Colorado but already missed you and them terribly."

"And?"

"I desperately started thinking of places I could hide from everyone. The next thing I knew I was sneaking back into the house, gathering up some clothes and supplies and stuffing them in my backpack."

"So, you're saying this was a spur of the moment move?"

Julie shrugged. "Well, not exactly, because I thought a lot about it the night before, but I didn't decide for sure until I was trying to tell Shasta and Jazz goodbye."

"I imagine you stopped by the kitchen and grabbed a few things as well."

Julie smiled. "As a matter of fact, I did. How'd you know?"

"Good guess, I suppose. Tell me this, weren't you afraid of being out there alone?"

"Uncle Mark, I had Shasta, Jazzy, and Brutus with me. What could go wrong?"

He rolled his eyes. "Just about everything. But worst of all, you didn't tell me you were going, and that was a thoughtless thing to do to someone who's responsible for you."

She hung her head. When she looked up, she had tears in her eyes, "I was selfish and should have known it was no way to solve the problem."

He was curious. "How far did you get?"

"I don't know exactly, but we traveled pretty fast, hoping to avoid anyone that might be looking for us."

Mark shook his head. "No wonder my men couldn't find you. They thought you'd be within five miles of the ranch, and we didn't know which way you'd gone. They missed a day of work doing that."

"I said I was sorry. I'll work extra hard this next month to make up for it."

"Don't be silly, Julie. I have another question. Your backpack is small, so how did you take food."

She laughed. "That was easy. Jazz has been carrying a pack for a while, because I've been trying to get him used to having weight on his back. I just loaded it up with water, peanut butter, crackers, and apples. I didn't have any food for the horses, so I gave them my apples."

"You were definitely prepared, at least for a day. Where did you stay that night?"

"We found a cave big enough to hold all four of us. I slept on my saddle blanket and put my coat over me. I didn't sleep much, because I thought something might spook the horses, and they'd step on me. And, fortunately, Brutus snuggled up against me, so I didn't get too cold."

Mark conceded, "Yes, I guess that was an adventure, but a dangerous one."

Julie added, "And in case you were wondering, I had a rope on

Jazzy when we left the ranch. He'd follow us when he was young, but he's two now, and I was afraid he'd go off on his own."

Mark smiled. "I think you were right."

That evening, as Mark was doing dishes, and Julie was drying, she said with a sigh, "I never realized such a big dark cloud has been hanging over me. I was afraid someday Aunt Fran would make me go back to Florida. But now I feel so free; I can hardly believe it. I can stay here forever, and no one can do anything about it."

Mark looked over and gave her a wink. "Unless I kick you out."

She frowned and nudged him with her hip. "I know better than that. By the way, how did you think of all those things you said to Aunt Fran? You were awesome."

He smiled. "It had to be God. I strayed from him long ago but asked him for help, and he was there for me."

"Does this mean you'll come sit beside me in church, instead of just dropping me off?"

He laughed. "Do I have to?"

She pouted. "I was hoping ..."

He nudged her back and smiled. "I guess I will. What a hardship—going to church, sitting next to someone I love, and learning about the creator of the universe and his Son."

She grinned and finished drying the dishes. Julie was pleased with his answer.

CHAPTER 13
Julie Rides Black Jazz for the first time

THE DAYS SPED by, until one day Julie said, "It's almost Christmas, and you know what that means?"

Her uncle looked at her quizzically.

"You told me I had to wait until Jazz was three before I could try riding him."

He grinned. "You don't say. I didn't know you were counting."

"You know I've been waiting and have been marking off the days on the calendar. The twenty-fifth of December is circled in red."

"I thought you were just excited about Christmas and Santa Claus coming."

She looked exasperated. "Uncle Maaaaarrk …"

He looked at her and grinned. "To tell you the truth, I didn't think you'd wait this long. I'm proud of you for not bugging me about riding that horse of yours."

"Well, it's been hard to see him every day and not want to get on him."

"How about we saddle him up after church tomorrow. I'm not usually a betting man, but let's bet whether or not he tries to buck you off after you get on him."

Julie said, "Okay. I say he doesn't actually buck, though I know he'll be uncomfortable, because it'll be strange to him."

Mark laughed and countered, "For the sake of argument, I bet he bucks and tries to scrape you off on a fence post."

Julie was excited. "You're on! What shall we bet?"

Her uncle responded immediately. "Let's bet back rubs. You'll give me four back rubs if he bucks and tries to get you off him. I'll give *you* the back rubs if he doesn't dump you."

"Sounds fine to me."

He laughed. "But if you're bucked off and end up in the dirt, *you'll* be the one who'll really needs the rubs."

Julie responded confidently, "Not going to happen."

Christmas Day was cloudy and cold, but by the time church was out, the clouds were starting to burn off. Mark looked up at the sky as he got out of the truck and quipped, "Looks like a great day for a rodeo." When they got to the barn, both horses were looking out of their stalls and neighed a welcome.

Julie sang "Happy Birthday" to Jazz and gave him his apple first, then she moved on to Shasta. As she patted the mare's muzzle she whispered, "I hope you've been telling Jazz to go easy on me today." What she got in return was a soft nicker.

Julie turned to her colt. "Today's the big day, Jazz. No fuss when I get on you, got that?"

She replaced his halter with a bridle then led him to an open area to saddle him. He gave her no trouble, probably because she'd been strapping packs on him for quite a while, so he was used to having weight on his back. She just wasn't sure how he'd react to having *her* on his back.

When they got outside, Mark held the bridle while Julie mounted. Jazz grunted and pranced sideways but didn't buck.

Jazz thought, *Why is she on my back? I'm not sure I like this,* but he didn't cause a ruckus because he knew it was Julie.

After a minute or two Julie signaled her uncle to let go of the bridle, and he backed away. Jazz snorted and backed up but still didn't buck, which made Julie smile. She thought back to all the time she'd spent getting him used to the bridle, putting weights in the saddlebags, and teaching him simple commands like stop. It had been worth it.

Uncle Mark shook his head and commented, "I guess I owe you four back rubs, Jules. What did you say to keep him calm?"

She laughed. "I promised him you'd give him the four back rubs I'd win if he was a good boy." They both laughed.

Julie spent the next hour on Jazz, training him to neck rein, because she hadn't been able to teach him neck reining on the lunge line. He was a quick learner, which pleased her immensely. She asked, "Uncle Mark, can we ride on a trail tomorrow? Look how well Jazz is doing."

"Whoa there, Julie. Let's give him a day or two to get him used to carrying you. I have some time on Wednesday. If you can wait until then, you, me, Shasta, and Jazz can explore a little. I don't think we should trust him out on the longer trails with other horses just yet."

On Wednesday, Jazz was a little skittish, but that was to be expected. He hadn't been in wide-open spaces except for their recent overnight adventure. When they got to a long and wide-open section of the trail, where other riders liked to race their horses, Uncle Mark turned to his niece. "Would you like to try a little run on Jazz? I'm not sure if he's fast or not, but it could be fun, provided you can stop him."

"Oh, I can stop him. He knows the command and what it means when I pull back on the reins."

"Okay, on the count of three, let's go."

When Mark reached three, they both gave their horses a swift kick. Shasta bolted forward, and Jazz bolted sideways in confusion, because he'd never gone faster than a trot with someone on his back. Julie wasn't expecting the lightning quick turn and almost fell off. Badly shaken, she grabbed the saddle horn and pulled herself upright. She wasn't used to riding a horse that bolted. Shasta and the other horses at Outfitters were calm. Even gunshots didn't bother them.

She leaned forward and whispered, "Jazz, it was my fault, and my sliding sideways probably scared you even more. I promise I'll be more careful, but at least I didn't fall off. That would've really scared you."

Uncle Mark heard the commotion almost immediately and whirled Shasta around to see what was going on. When he saw Julie clinging to the side of her saddle he panicked "Are you okay? I heard you scream, and it scared me." He was shaking. "Why don't we go back to the ranch, because you look shaken up."

Julie reassured him. "I'm okay. I let my guard down, which was very stupid of me. I'll be more careful next time. It wasn't Jazz's fault; it was mine. I wasn't paying attention like I should have been." She grinned. "Actually, *you* look more shaken up than I do."

Once Julie was settled firmly in the saddle, they continued their ride—but slower. Later, they came upon a fast-moving stream. Julie thought Jazz would balk at the crossing, but he didn't. He slogged his way right through it, probably remembering running along behind his mom on earlier rides when he was a young colt. He'd always hesitated at water crossings but ended up plunging across to keep up.

When they got back to the ranch, it was time to rub the horses down as a reward for a good ride. Being brushed was Jazz's favorite activity, outside of eating apples.

CHAPTER 14
Introduction to Rodeos

AS TIME WENT by, their treks into the wilderness became more frequent. Sometimes they went with a group on overnight trips, but Jazz wasn't crazy about the overnight rides. He preferred his warm, safe stall at night, but he didn't complain and balk, because Julie was always his rider. He liked having her close by.

One day, a rather large man came to the ranch and began looking the horses over. He spied Jazz in a paddock on the far side of Barn 2 and wanted to ride him. With a loud voice he ordered, "Bring that one out. I want to look at him."

The stable hand told him he was a privately owned horse, so it was unavailable.

"Nonsense. I just want to see him."

He brought Jazz out from his paddock, knowing the man couldn't rent him, but he'd been so insistent on seeing the horse he didn't want to make him mad.

When Jazz was brought out, he seemed to drag the ranch hand along with him. The man commented, "Spunky, isn't he?"

"Yes, sir, but he's not for rent."

He demanded, "But *that's* the one I want!"

"Sorry, sir."

The man whirled around, got in his truck, and left. When they told Julie what had happened, she laughed. She already knew her Friesian was impressive, but she was sorry Uncle Mark had lost a customer.

Jules was pleased the man liked her horse. She knew he was beautiful, but maybe she'd been taking him for granted. That afternoon she watched him in the paddock. He was sleek and black, and his muscles rippled as he moved in the sunlight. His neck arched proudly when he pranced by, and his mane was now almost two feet long, the same length as his mother's. His wavy tail seemed to float behind him as he ran, and it nearly touched the ground. "Yes, my pretty Jazz, you're a beautiful horse, and I'm very glad you're mine." Jazz nodded his head as if he understood. Julie knew why that man admired and wanted to ride him. He was special.

While Mark was fixing dinner that evening, Julie told him all about the man who'd been so impressed by Jazz. He commented, "Jules, have you ever thought you might like to take him to the rodeo in Denver? It would be fun, and Jazz might do great in the western pleasure class, or even in barrel racing. He may need some training, but I think he'd surprise you. He'd certainly be a beautiful entrant."

"What other training could he possibly need? He walks, trots, canters, and stops. What more is there?"

He looked over at her. "Mrs. Reynolds, who lives down the road, often shows her horses at the rodeos that come to Denver. She might be able to give you some pointers, like how to teach Jazz to be more responsive to your signals and change leads when he changes direction."

She replied, "It can't be *that* hard, but I'll give her a call."

The next week Julie went to see her and was surprised at how much more her horse needed to know to be competitive. She told Julie to always call her Ruth, because calling her Mrs. Reynolds made her feel old. Julie assured her she could do that. Then she explained the various rodeo events that might be a good fit for her and Jazz.

First, she mentioned barrel racing. "Lots of women like to compete in barrel racing, but I'm sure you already know all about that event."

Julie looked embarrassed. "I'm afraid I don't know *anything* about barrel racing, or any other rodeo event. I was raised in Florida, near the beach, so I know more about surfboards than I do about horses or rodeos."

Ruth looked surprised. "Well, I guess I'll have to explain some of the events you might find interesting. Here goes. Barrel racing is a timed event where the riders race on a course consisting of three barrels set in triangular, or 'cloverleaf' pattern. Riders can choose to circle the first barrel either clockwise or counterclockwise. They usually choose the direction based on the lead their horse finds most comfortable. But sometimes a rider wants to tell the horse which lead to use, depending on the direction they are turning."

Ruth noticed Julie's quizzical look. "Don't worry, I'll explain leads in a minute." She continued, "After circling the first barrel, a rider races to the opposite barrel and circles it. After they've circled the third barrel, they race to the finish line. Oh, I forgot to mention, knocking over a barrel carries a five-second penalty, though some rodeos give the rider a 'no time' mark for that error." She continued. "Occasionally, a rider may hit the barrel, but not tip it over. That's okay. The crowd thinks cutting it close is a good thing, because it could shave time off the run."

"Do the racers have to get a fast start so their time will be better?"

"Julie, that's a great question. Barrel racers kick-start their horses in the alley leading to the starting line, so they'll be at full speed when they go through the timer. That's only fair, because some horses are just not that fast off a starting line."

Jules sounded discouraged. "Are there any events less complicated than barrel racing? Something I can do without too much training?"

"Well, there's the western pleasure class, which is a competition that basically evaluates horses on their manners. The aim is to show the horse and rider are relaxed and can maintain a collected gait at a slow speed. The horse must also display a calm and responsive attitude; in other words, he must look like he's a pleasure to ride. The ride should be both comfortable and smooth."

Julie asked, "Does it matter what the horse looks like?"

"Appearance is also evaluated, but maybe not in the way you think. Horses that are calm, quiet, and have collected gaits that demonstrate the required slow, controlled movements are what the judges are looking for. Those horses may outscore a pretty horse. Judges also prefer to see a loosely draped rein at all times. A horse that prances and swishes its tail on a tighter rein may be pretty and look spirited, but that won't cut it in this competition. Many judges think those actions may be signs of a rebellious horse."

"Ruth, Jazz is pretty, and often prances when he walks. Would that look bad to the judges?

"It shouldn't matter if your horse's natural gait is a little flashy. Judges take that into consideration, but they like seeing your horse under control, with little effort on your part. Sometimes there are events in this class that group horses like Friesians, Arabians, and other spirited horses together, so they can judge them without penalizing them for their showy action."

Julie thought for a minute. "Can we go back to the *lead* thing you were talking about? How would I know my horse is on the right lead?"

Ruth looked around. "Did you ride over on your horse?"

"I did."

"Good. Take him to the corral behind the barn, and I can watch you ride him in a few figure eights. Some horses just naturally change leads when they change directions. Basically, when a horse is using the correct lead, the inside front and hind legs reach farther forward than the outside legs. If he's turning left, he should be putting his left foot forward first, and vice versa. Horses are better balanced when they are on the correct lead."

Julie performed figure eights while Ruth watched. Much to her surprise, Ruth commented, "Julie, you're lucky because not all horses naturally change leads like Jazz does. He looked beautiful and fluid on every turn."

"Whew, I was afraid I was going to have to teach him something hard. You saw him in a canter. What about in a trot?"

"No lead changes in a trot—just in a canter, or a lope. Sometime cowboys use the term *lope* instead of canter, but they're the same thing. After watching Jazz, it looks like you're all set." Ruth reassured her. "Don't worry, I'll tell you if I ever see him using the incorrect lead."

Julie breathed a sigh of relief. "Thanks. At least I don't have to teach him that. What events do you think we'd be good in?"

"Barrel racing takes lots of practice. In that event, some of the competitors have been racing most of their lives. If you really think you might be interested, I can set up some barrels for you so you can try running them."

Julie said, "Not today, but thank you." She couldn't stay because she had to be home early tonight, but she *was* interested. She knew there'd be plenty of time for her to practice, because she probably wouldn't try barrel racing until next year. Before she left, she told Ruth the western pleasure class was more her speed right now, and Ruth agreed.

When she got home, she asked her uncle when the next rodeo in the Denver area was scheduled.

He just looked at her over the rim of his reading glasses. "Unless your arms are broken, go upstairs and Google it yourself." He winked at her and then returned to his reading.

CHAPTER 15
Exploring the Fairgrounds

JULIE TOLD HER uncle the next National Western Stock Show in Denver was only two months away. When he saw she was serious about entering the pleasure class, he offered to sign her up online. A few days later he had another suggestion. "Why don't I sign you up to ride in the rodeo parade, too. It should be fun, and you'd get to meet others who are going to compete against you."

Julie sounded excited. "The parade sounds great!"

Before she could say more, he winced and added, "And you could carry a banner with Estes Park Wilderness Outfitters on it." Then he chuckled. "Or put a big sign on your back."

"Uncle Maaark, you've got to be kidding me."

"Nope, lots of people in the parade advertise their businesses. I could ride Shasta right next to you. What a striking pair we'd make—two beautiful black prancing Friesians, and a pretty young woman." He added, "I was just kidding about putting a sign on your back."

Julie weakened. "Well, I guess I'll go if you go with me—but only if *you* hold the banner."

He laughed all the way upstairs to his room. While he was getting ready for bed, he thanked God for bringing such a sweet little sprite into his life.

The next few days, Julie worked hard to teach Jazz to be more responsive to her signals. She used the reins, her heels, and legs to tell him what she needed him to do. It was difficult for him at first, because he was full of life and found it more fun to be spirited. She started patting his neck and leaning down to give him treats when he stayed calm. It seemed to work, so she felt they were almost ready for the competition.

Uncle Mark had entered Julie in the western pleasure class, but first they had to ride in the rodeo parade. That would be a test of how Jazz would act around crowds and strange horses, especially other stallions.

Julie was amazed at how well her horse behaved in the parade. Though he pranced and tossed his head, he stayed in line and didn't act up. Mark was next to them on Shasta, which may have kept him calm. They saw lots of people, especially kids, pointing and saying, "Look at the pretty horses." She knew he looked good, but she still loved to hear it. Uncle Mark had convinced her *she* should carry the Estes Park Wilderness Outfitters banner, by saying people would pay more attention to the sign if a pretty girl held it. He had bought her a flag boot so she could rest the end of the flagpole in her stirrup, so it wasn't heavy at all.

The parade finished up indoors and circled the arena. The crowd cheered wildly, and Julie was in heaven. She was on a beautiful horse and was about to compete in her first rodeo event.

***

After the parade, they put Shasta and Jazz in their stalls then went outside to explore the fairgrounds. There were booths everywhere, offering everything from fried pickles to funnel cakes. Then they moved inside to check out the exhibits. There were political booths, truck dealerships, and any other products you could possibly buy at a fair. Julie noticed a booth in the corner. As they walked toward it, she asked her uncle, "What is a therapeutic riding center?"

Mark wasn't sure. "Let's go ask."

They were met with a handshake and a warm smile. Julie asked, "What does this type of riding center do?"

Janice Reamy, a lady at the booth, was happy to tell them. "Our program has been helping individuals with special needs for years. We were founded so they, especially children, could experience a quality of life change through being around horses. We use very special horses, which actually become four-legged therapists."

Uncle Mark commented, "I've heard of using dogs for therapy—you know, using them to provide affection and comfort to people in hospitals, nursing homes, etc. —but never horses." He bent down and whispered to Julie, "Probably because they won't fit in their laps." She giggled.

Ms. Reamy continued as if she hadn't heard the interruption, but Mark didn't mind because he could tell she was passionate about the subject. "Riding for special-needs children is an entire body experience, because it touches the kids' emotions as well. For example, imagine you are always in a wheelchair, but when you get on a horse, you sit high enough so most people are not looking down at you. Wouldn't that rock your world? It sure does for the handicapped. Just think about how excited and powerful you'd feel if you were able to control a big animal like a horse, when you've never been able to control anything, not even your legs? We love our riding center."

Julie picked up their brochures and thanked Ms. Reamy for telling them about their organization.

Mark looked at his watch. "Jules, we better get crackin'. It's time to get Jazzy warmed up for your event."

***

As it turned out, Jazz didn't win the pleasure riding event, but Julie was still pleased because she'd taken third place and she was eager to hang the ribbon in her room. Not bad for her first time out. She thought Jazz performed great, but as Ruth said, sometimes judges are not fond of spirited horses in that class. It's not that he didn't respond to her commands, but he was a showoff and pranced a bit, and his trot was lively, to say the least. Oh, well, maybe this would never be his best event, but she'd have him ready for barrel racing next year.

Julie was very quiet on the way back to Estes Park, so Mark asked, "You aren't disappointed because you came in third place, are you?"

"No."

She was still quiet, so he asked, "Jules, are you sick, or do you have something on your mind?"

"I've been thinking about the therapeutic riding center, that's all. It seems like a very worthwhile cause. Do we have anything like that in Estes Park?"

Mark shook his head. "I've not heard of one." He looked over at her. "So that's what's on your mind?"

"I guess so—the riding center," but she said no more.

After they put the horses away and brushed and fed them, she went up to her room, opened her laptop, and Googled "therapeutic riding." The more she read about it, the more she thought they needed such a center in the mountains.

After lunch the next day, Julie asked her uncle a question. "Uncle Mark, I've not used any of the money I received from Mom and Dad's settlement, have I?"

"No, you haven't, and neither have I. You're my responsibility, so I shouldn't be paid to keep you. Why do you ask?"

"I was wondering if I had enough money to start one of those centers—you know, a therapeutic riding center?"

He'd known something was on her mind, but he had no idea it would be this. "You have more than enough money, but why would you think about doing that?"

"There are handicapped people up here in the mountains, too. We enjoy our horses so much, and I think it would be nice to let the kids be around horses and maybe ride them."

He walked over and put his arms around her. "My sweet Jules, that would be a nice and thoughtful thing to do, but we don't know the first thing about that kind of program. You can't learn everything on the internet, and I'm sure the center would have to be certified. They can't just let anyone plop a handicapped child on a pony and tell them to hold on."

She responded, "Maybe we can visit one of those centers and see what it's all about."

He shook his head, not believing she was interested in such a center, but said, "You find a place to visit, and we'll go."

She clapped excitedly. "Thank you, thank you, Uncle Mark," then gave him one of those hugs he hated so much.

CHAPTER 16
Visiting a Therapeutic Riding Center

A FEW WEEKS later they visited the Denver center featured in the brochure. She liked the place but wanted to see others so they could get more ideas. She found one that sounded interesting on the internet. It was the American Therapeutic Riding Center in Sand Springs, Oklahoma. "Uncle Mark, if you aren't too busy, can we go there next week?"

"We sure can, kiddo, but I'll have to check my schedule first." The next week they were on their way to Oklahoma.

As they drove onto the facility grounds in Sand Springs, Julie commented, "This state is very different from Colorado. Here they only have rolling hills and not nearly as many trees."

They met with the director, and because there was so much to remember, they took notes. It was soon evident they needed to talk with others as soon as they got back to Estes Park. The first thing she needed to find out was if there was even a need in the Estes Park area for such a place. Their heads were swimming with questions as the director talked.

Mark leaned over to Julie and whispered, "At least we already know we have room at the ranch for a center, so we won't have to buy more land." She smiled.

They took a walking tour of the center and were amazed at all the special apparatus needed to handle handicapped riders. Julie raised her hand and asked, "So, would we need all this equipment?"

The director answered, "Yes. And you'll need horses specifically trained for therapy work. The list of the training the horses must have to do this kind of therapy is very long."

Julie moved closer to her uncle and whispered, "I didn't know it took this much effort to start one of these centers."

He glanced down at her. "We have lots to discuss while we drive home, but for right now, you need to pay attention to what she's saying. It's important if you're really serious about setting up a center like this."

Julie stifled a yawn as the director continued to describe the type of horses they would need. She finally heard her say to the people listening, "In closing, our instructors should be certified with the Certified Horsemanship Association (CHA) or the Professional Association of Therapeutic Horsemanship International (PATH). You can post an ad with CHA or PATH to find certified instructors."

She smiled at the crowd. "I have much more to tell you about our center, but this should give you an overview of what you are looking at if you want to start a center like this yourself. I hope I haven't discouraged you."

Julie thought, *Thank goodness she's done. I'm glad she told us about the center, but now I'm depressed.*

They both thanked her then headed for the truck. Julie spoke first. "I didn't know it would be this complicated. It would take a million people to get one of these centers going."

Mark laughed. "Well, not quite a million, but it would certainly take more than the two of us."

"Where would we start? It seems impossible."

When they got settled in the truck, her uncle patted her leg. "Take it to the Lord tonight, Jules. You may not get the answer you expect, but you *will* get an answer—and have peace about whatever you decide."

She whined, "I'm not feeling peace right now."

Mark responded gently, "Do what I said, and we'll talk about it again tomorrow. I suggest you call around and get an estimate of how many handicapped children are actually in our area, because if there are just a few, you may want to alter your plans."

"That's a good idea. I really should have investigated before having you drive me all the way to Oklahoma. I know there are kids in Denver who need this kind of place, but we're seventy miles from Denver, and there are several centers closer for them to use."

That night Julie Googled therapeutic riding centers in Larimer County, Colorado. There were none. Then she printed off a list of facilities she could call tomorrow to get an estimate of how many handicapped children were within twenty-five miles of Estes Park. When she'd heard from all of them, she realized there really wasn't a need for such a center in her county.

She reported what she found to Uncle Mark. "I'm glad there aren't many handicapped children who live around here, but now I know there really isn't a need for what I want to do."

"Isn't that an answer to your prayers? Now you know you need to find other ways to serve your community."

Julie was discouraged. "But what else can I do? I really thought this was a good idea."

Uncle Mark looked sympathetic. "Surely there are other ways to help people. I'm not going to give you ideas because you need to let God give you a path."

CHAPTER 17
Barrel Racing

JULIE DIDN'T WANT to sit around and mope, so she rode over to see Ruth. When Julie saw her, she asked, "What do you have planned for this beautiful fall day?"

Without hesitation Ruth responded, "I have Dusty coming over. He's my friend who's great at barrel racing. You're welcome to stay if you want."

When Dusty drove in pulling his trailer, they both walked out to meet him. Ruth spoke first. "Glad to see you made it. I think it's supposed to rain the next couple of days, and that'll keep you from riding, so unload Rex then come in and grab a quick bite of lunch before you run the barrels."

Over lunch, Julie asked Dusty questions about barrel racing. "How did you get started in barrel racing? What kind of horses are best in your event? Do they use stopwatches to time the riders?"

"Whoa, girl! Ask me one question at a time. I believe you asked me how I got started in barrel racing. Well, I was the youngest, and the *only* boy in the family. My sisters barrel raced so I joined in, thinking I could beat them for sure. But it wasn't until recently my time was better than theirs."

He laughed and added, "Another reason was I was too chicken to bronc or bull ride, but don't tell anyone I said that."

He thought a minute. "Let's see, I believe your second question was what kind of horses are best in this sport. My horse, Rex, is a quarter horse, so I'm partial to that breed. They have those big, strong hindquarters, so there's plenty of power to get you around the barrels fast. Old Rex is quick, but other breeds can turn in good times too—*if* they have the right training and rider."

Julie interrupted. "And how do they time the event?"

Dusty leaned back in his chair as he explained. "Good question. We get a fast start by getting up to speed in the alley leading to the arena. At the starting line, we cross an electronic beam, which is a timer, and it keeps running until we cross it again at the end of the run. That's why riders run in and out of the arena as fast as they can. They want to hit the beam going full speed in both directions."

Julie started to ask another question. "How come—"

Dusty interrupted her. "Enough questions for now. We're burning daylight, and I need to saddle up and practice. Ruth said rain's expected tomorrow, so we can't waste the good weather."

Once outside, Julie watched him saddle Rex then head for the corral. She thought, *What a pretty horse. And Dusty was right, quarter horses have big, powerful hindquarters.*

Ruth knew Dusty would be practicing barrel racing today, so she'd had her stable hands put out three fifty-five-gallon plastic drums. When Rex saw the barrels, he started prancing, knowing exactly what he had to do. He was itching to run, but Dusty held him back. "Yup, he's pretty eager, but first we need to make sure the barrels are in the right places." He looked over at Julie and explained, "They are placed in a triangle. Usually there's ninety feet between barrel one and barrel two, 105 feet between barrels one and three and two and three, and it's sixty feet from the two closest barrels to the finish line. Some rodeos with larger arenas change those distances a little, but most use these dimensions, so that's how we practice."

Julie watched as Dusty lined his horse up, ready to start. Rex was a beautiful chestnut gelding with a blaze and four white stockings.

When he kick-started Rex, she could see the four white feet go into action, becoming a blur in the dust he churned up. Julie cheered as he circled barrels one, two and three, then ran flat out to the finish line. When Rex stopped, Dusty whirled around toward the two women and tipped his hat to show he appreciated their cheering.

As he got closer, he grinned. "That felt pretty good. Too bad no one timed it."

Julie smiled up at him. "Impressive, but I expected a good show from a horse named Rex, because Rex means king. I wasn't disappointed."

Dusty was surprised. "I didn't know that's what his name meant, but it fits, doesn't it?" Proudly he said, "Rex is the king of barrel racing horses."

Ruth teased. "Don't you wish? But I have to admit it was a spectacular ride."

As usual, Julie had a question. "Ruth, I notice your barrels are made of plastic. Don't they tip over easier than metal ones?"

Ruth answered, "Sure they do. Most rodeos use metal barrels because they're heavier and more durable. Some would use plastic barrels because they are easier to move, but the rules don't allow them to put weights in the bottom to keep them from tipping easily." Ruth added, "We practice with the plastic barrels for two reasons: one, they're easier to move around, and two, they are easier to tip. We'd rather our horses learn to avoid even touching them."

Julie looked thoughtful. "That makes sense."

Dusty looked over at Julie. "Do you want to try running the barrels with Jazz? It's fun, but don't expect too much from him at first. Getting around those barrels without tipping them over takes practice. Give it a shot."

Julie mounted Jazz and entered the corral. He was curious about the barrels, so she slowly circled them, letting him sniff each one as much as he wanted. When he seemed to lose interest, she took him back to the place where Dusty had started.

She leaned over, patted his neck, and spoke softly. "Jazzy, I know this is new to you, but let's try it and see how you do."

Julie gathered her reins, leaned forward, then gave him a firm kick. When they got to the first barrel, she tried reining him around the barrel, but he was confused. He wasn't used to turning quickly when he still had room to run. It was obvious to Ruth and Dusty he was fighting her. The second barrel was the same. Jazz found the barrels puzzling. He'd always run *by* things in his way, not around them. The third barrel was easier, because once he finished his circle, he was given his head to race flat out to the finish line with nothing to stop him.

Dusty was laughing when Julie pulled up in front of him. She frowned and spoke sharply. "So, Dusty, is your laughing supposed to encourage me?"

He tried to hide his smile. "Please understand, I'm not laughing to embarrass you, but you two were quite a sight going around those barrels. I think once Jazz figures out what he's supposed to do, you'll be amazed at how well he does. The first time is always the worst."

"Really?" she said hopefully. "I know we were was pretty bad."

"He'll get better, and so will you. Trust me."

By the end of the day Julie could see progress. Jazz no longer rebelled when guided around the turns, because he was starting to understand. She knew when he began treating racing around the barrels like a game, he'd be a great barrel horse.

The next few days were dreary and wet, so no one rode. Julie was sad and looked wistfully out the window. "I sure wish we had somewhere dry we could ride on days like this."

Mark overheard her and commented, "I don't know of any indoor rings in the area, do you?"

"Nope." She plodded slowly to her room to check her email. When she sat down, she thought of the center she had hoped to build, and how disappointed she was it had turned out to be a bad idea. A few minutes later she began Googling indoor riding rings to learn more about them.

CHAPTER 18
Second Thoughts

WHEN SHE WENT downstairs, she sprawled out on a chair near Mark. "Do you think we have enough room here for a riding arena, so we can ride indoors on days like this? It's depressing not to be able to ride when it's raining."

He looked surprised. "I don't know why you even have to ask, since a therapeutic riding center would've had one. You *know* we have room here for whatever you want to build. Remember, I own more than two hundred acres, although I admit some of it is on the side of a mountain."

"Would a person need flat land to build an arena?"

"Not necessarily. Engineers blast into mountainsides, and build up valleys, to make a flat space for structures, all the time."

"Do you think people around here would use a place like an indoor arena?"

He paused a minute. "I do. Our riding is very restricted in bad weather, especially when there's a lot of snow on the ground. That's pretty often here in Colorado. I think it'd be a *very* valuable asset to the community."

"Would you ever use it?"

He answered truthfully, "Maybe not me, but I know there are

people in the area who'd love to have a place where their kids could ride in the winter, or when it's raining."

He thought for a minute. "And people who rodeo would love to have a place to practice year-round. You know as well as I do, Colorado is rough in the winter. Think about your friend Dusty. He can't work his horse on the barrels if the weather's bad, or even if it's recently rained. Too slippery and dangerous."

"So you think an indoor riding arena would be a good idea?"

"Absolutely. Not many of us have the money to fulfill a dream like that, but you do. I'd say thanks to your parents' accident, you have the money, but I'm sure you'd rather have them back than money for a riding arena."

"I would *definitely* rather have them back, but I do treasure what I've found here with you in Colorado. I never would have even known you existed."

Her uncle admitted, "That's probably true, but maybe not."

Julie was thoughtful. "I was really hoping to start one of those centers, because it would've helped handicapped kids."

"Julie, look at it this way. We only have two or three kids in this area who *may* have been able to use the center. With an indoor arena, you'd be serving the entire community, both children and adults. In the long run, which is a better investment? The Lord says we must be wise stewards of our money, and I believe spending thousands of dollars for the good of many is probably better than putting the same amount into serving a few. I'm sure you'll find other ways to serve those kids, even though it won't be with a big therapeutic riding center like you saw in Denver or in Oklahoma."

Julie thought about it a minute. "I guess you're right, but I still want to pray about it."

Her uncle responded, "Of course, and you should. I wouldn't advise you to skip that important step, because this is a very big decision, and it would be a huge investment."

***

In a few weeks winter would creep into Estes Park. The air was nippy, and on some mornings there was already ice in the puddles. Julie knew they wouldn't start building the arena until spring, so she and her uncle used their spare time to go over plans and research contractors they might use for the structure.

Online, Julie found the dimensions of a rodeo arena that could handle roping, barrel racing, and other riding events. It would need to be approximately 140 feet by 240 feet, plus room for stands, so people could watch what was going on in the ring.

Her uncle asked, "Do you want to include a covered area for stalls, grooming areas, and chutes for the broncs?"

Julie whined, "That sounds like a *big* rodeo facility. I just want a place for folks around here to ride when the weather's bad. We don't need all the things you mentioned."

Uncle Mark made a suggestion. "If people have to stay overnight because of weather, or if they've come from a distance, you might want a covered area with a few stalls. My barns can hold one or two extra horses, but not many more than that."

Julie agreed. "I guess you're right, but I don't want to take up too much of your land."

"Don't worry about that. I have plenty of room, but as you mentioned the other day, it would be more economical to build the complex where the land is fairly flat. We'll check it out tomorrow."

CHAPTER 19
Community Response to
Indoor Riding Center

THE DAYS SEEMED to fly by. Soon Christmas arrived, which meant another party for Jazz. After passing the apples and sugar out to the two horses, Julie and her uncle walked back to the house. Once inside, she noticed the blinking answering machine. She played the message. "Julie, this is Sarah from the Rocking W Ranch down the road, I understand you may be building an indoor riding center at your uncle's ranch. We are *so* excited. I'm sure it'll cost a fortune, so we'd like to help. I've told lots of people in the area, and they want to contribute as well. Give me a call and let me know if there's anything we can do, including donating money toward the construction. Bye."

Julie shouted for Mark. She sounded so panicked he ran to find her. "What's the matter? Are you okay?"

All she said was, "Listen to this."

He was just as shocked as she had been and apologized. "Jules, honest, I only told one person you were considering building an indoor arena. I emphasized the word *considering* when I told Jeff. He must have burned up the wires calling everyone he knew. I had no idea he'd spread the word."

She laughed. "I guess now that everyone knows, we're locked into building it."

He smiled. "I don't think everyone knowing is what convinced you. You decided to go ahead with this project weeks ago."

"You're right, but it's kind of exciting that people want to be a part of it."

Mark didn't hesitate. "Looks like you're going to have to call a meeting so you can find out exactly what *contribute* means. It might just mean having bake sales to help raise money, which is

okay. I'm just blown away that the people around here want to help."

***

The first person Julie contacted about the get-together, told her she ought to make it a potluck. She added, when you call people, ask them to bring themselves and good food to share.

During the meeting, Julie stood up and asked everyone to be quiet, because she had an announcement to make. "This project will be called the H-K Indoor Riding Center, which stands for Hubbard-Kasting."

Mark, who was in shock, looked over at her and mouthed a silent "thank you." She was amazed when people crowded around and started handing her checks, for as little as a few dollars to several thousand, just to get the project started.

She knew Estes Park had attracted people from all over the United States, because it was quaint and beautiful, but now she saw the warmth and generosity of its people.

When the group left the lodge, she turned to her uncle. "I had no idea people around here would be so generous and eager to have an indoor arena. We'd better get serious about this and choose a contractor, so we can get started this spring."

Before going up to bed, they talked quietly in front of the fire. "Uncle Mark, I feel peace about this project. I didn't feel peace about the other one."

"That's what it's all about, Jules. God lets us know when we're on the right track."

The next afternoon, Julie brought her laptop downstairs and asked Mark if he'd look through the plans she'd found. "Look at this one. It's huge and looks like a long white tent or a greenhouse. It would provide lots of light, which I like."

Mark commented, "It looks nice, and seems to be less expensive than others we've looked at, but remember, this is Estes Park, Colorado, and we have low temperatures and lots of snow here. Though this arena is beautiful, it probably wouldn't stand up to our climate. And I imagine an arena like this would be quite cold inside, because there'd be no way to insulate it. It would cost a fortune to heat."

"You're right."

Together they looked through many designs and finally decided on a pole and beam structure that had a fully insulated tin roof, with several skylights down its length. There were also many windows on each side, to not only let in light, but fresh air in the summertime. It took them several weeks to decide on a plan, leaving Julie both excited and exhausted.

***

The whole town was invited to the groundbreaking ceremony the day construction began. People were happy the project was getting started, but the animals in the nearby barns were quite upset when bulldozers started leveling the area. The horses soon grew used to the noise—all except Jazz. He didn't like it one bit, probably because the construction was about fifty yards from his small paddock. He whinnied, snorted, and plunged around, tossing his head like a swarm of bees was after him. Julie tried to calm him, but he'd have none of it. He wanted that noise and dust gone *now*. But it still was a beautiful sight to see him run back and forth in the paddock all day long.

One day, one of the workers, Bruce Nolan, sitting on a nearby bulldozer, noticed Jazz and thought, *What a beautiful horse that is. I'd like to have that big guy.* He stopped and watched him many times a day, hoping he'd have a chance to at least touch him. One afternoon, Mike Larson, the foreman, noticed his interest and told him to get back to work.

The next day Bruce heard a loud voice behind him. "How many times have I told you to leave that horse alone. Did I see you throwing something at him? I hope not."

"Boss, it was just a few pebbles. I was trying to make him run because he looks so pretty in motion."

Mike could hardly believe what he'd heard and responded instantly. "I want to see *you* in motion. Get off this site, and I don't want to see you back here ever again, which means *you're fired!*"

"Boss, what about my paycheck?"

"I'll mail it to you. Go *now!*"

CHAPTER 20
Black Jazz Stolen

FIVE WEEKS LATER, the arena was finished, and the crew was gone. Mike walked through the structure with Julie and her uncle and asked, "Well, how do you like it?"

Julie gushed. "It's beautiful. I can hardly believe it's done, even the landscaping. Now we can invite our friends to a grand opening party. You're invited if you want to come."

He shook his head. "As much as I like a good party, I'm glad to be out of here. I had a little problem with one of my dozer operators, and it's still bothering me. But I hope you all have a great time and enjoy the arena."

They shook hands, then Julie excused herself and headed back to the lodge to start planning the celebration. It was going to be fun for everyone. She hoped the weather was good, but with the new arena, even rain couldn't dampen the festivities. They would have a roof over their heads and plenty of room to party. Hopefully, some folks would bring their horses and try out the complex, which now included several outbuildings for storing equipment.

The whole town came and loved it.

The day after the grand opening, Julie went to Barn 2 to check on Jazz. She wanted to ride him in the new arena, but didn't hear his familiar neigh as she entered the barn. She thought, *That's strange. Jazz always knows when I'm coming to see him.* She panicked when she found his stall empty. If she'd forgotten to latch the stall door, it would still be open, but it was latched tight. She ran out to the paddock and prayed he was there, but he wasn't. She raced to Barn 1 to see if one of the hands had let him out into the big pasture, but they hadn't. Immediately, she headed for the main lodge to find her uncle.

Mark was coming down the front steps when he saw his niece running toward him. "Where's the fire? You're sure in a rush."

She was out of breath, but managed to say, "Jazz is gone!"

He was concerned but not worried. Surely he was somewhere on the property. He asked, "And you've checked everywhere, even the pastures?"

Julie assured him the horse was nowhere to be found, and no one had seen him that morning.

Immediately, he pulled out his cell phone and called 911 to report Jazz missing. Estes Park was a horse town, so the sheriff's office knew the report was serious. Stealing a horse was a big offense.

Sheriff Brady McKnight immediately came to the phone. "Mark, this is Brady. Which horse is gone, and do you have any idea how long he's been missing?"

"Jazz is gone, and I have no idea when he was taken. No one around the barns noticed any strangers in the area, so I have to assume he was stolen in the middle of the night."

Within ten minutes, Barn 2 was swarming with deputies trying to find clues, and if they were lucky, tracks. Mark and Julie were asked, "Do you know of anyone who's shown an unusual interest in your horse?" They could think of no one, especially one who would steal a horse.

Thirty minutes later Mike Logan, their contractor, called. "I just heard about Jazz. The guy I fired a few weeks ago is the only person I can think of who might have taken your horse. His name is Bruce Nolan. I'll get his phone number and address for you."

After thanking Mike, he turned to Julie and the sheriff. "We may have a lead."

A squad car stopped by Nolan's apartment to question him, but no one was home.

Mark had called all his friends. They mounted up and then headed out to search the area. Three hours later they found Bruce Nolan in the woods, holding his shoulder and limping toward town.

A deputy asked, "Are you Bruce Nolan, and what happened to you?"

"I was out trying to find the horse you're looking for. I was lucky enough to get a rope on him, but he attacked me. As you can see, my shoulder is probably dislocated, and the stupid horse kicked me in the leg, so I had to let him go. I couldn't give him a chance to run at me again, so I let go of the rope."

"How long ago was this, and which way did he go?"

Bruce told him, "It was about five or six hours ago, and I think he headed north." They informed the other searchers, and all headed in that direction.

As soon as the police heard the news, they informed Mark and Julie. Mark thought for a minute. "Sheriff, when did we start our search? It was about three hours ago, wasn't it?"

The sheriff looked at his watch. "That sounds about right."

Mark reasoned, "Then how could this Nolan guy have started searching for Jazz five hours ago?"

The sheriff raised one eyebrow. "Good question. We need to talk to him and get some answers."

Meanwhile, the deputy sheriff who had spotted Nolan offered to give him a ride to the hospital in the squad car. He loudly complained the entire ride to the emergency room. "That horse tried to kill me, so something has to be done with him. I tell ya', he's a killer."

When the sheriff arrived at the hospital he asked, "Mr. Nolan, did you do anything to provoke the horse?"

"No. sir. I know better than that. I just got a rope on him, and he attacked."

"So you're positive you did nothing to the horse?"

Bruce replied immediately. "Not a thing. That horse is just loco."

The sheriff looked down at his notes and asked another question. "What time did you say the horse attacked you?"

"It was about nine o'clock this morning. Actually, I *know* it was nine o'clock because that devil kicked my watch, and now it's busted." He showed him his wrist. "See, my watch stopped at *exactly* nine, so I was telling you the truth."

He was asked again, "Are you sure you did nothing to provoke the horse?"

"No way. I already told you that. I know better than to do something that stupid to a horse running loose in the woods. I just tried to get a rope on him, so I could get him back to where he came from." Bruce lowered his voice and stepped closer to the sheriff. "Confidentially, I was hoping there might be some reward money involved; you know, for finding the horse and all."

The sheriff scratched his head. "Let's get this straight, Bruce. You said you were attacked at nine o'clock this morning, and you have a broken watch to prove it. Is that correct?"

Bruce answered decisively, "That's *exactly* right. And that's why I think that killer horse should be put down. He's vicious. I was just doing a good deed for someone, and look where it got me."

The sheriff turned to his deputy. "Brandon, what time did we receive the call notifying us Julie's horse was missing?"

The deputy looked down at the call register. "This report shows the call came in at 10:05 this morning."

"And what time did we gather at the Outfitters to start the search?"

The deputy answered, "It was around eleven o'clock by the time we determined the horse could not be found on Mr. Hubbard's property. Then we started the search."

The sheriff looked back at Bruce. "Do you see why there might be a problem here?"

Bruce shrugged, indicating he had no idea what the problem might be.

"You were attacked at nine o'clock, but we hadn't yet been notified the horse was missing. "Can you explain that?"

"I can't. I just know what happened." The nurse interrupted and informed Bruce the doctor was ready to see him.

The sheriff stepped back. "Okay, Mr. Nolan, that's all I have to ask you right now, but I'll probably have some questions later, so don't leave town."

Before he went with the nurse, Bruce pointed his finger at Mark and Julie, who'd been standing nearby. "And *your* outfit's going to pay all my hospital bills—and more—for having a dangerous animal loose where he could hurt someone."

When Bruce wasn't looking, the sheriff looked at Mark and rolled his eyes, then turned back and said, "Okay, Mr. Nolan, we'll see what happens." Then he winked at Julie.

Bruce gave everyone a big smile because he felt very important. They now *knew* he was a valuable witness, so maybe he could testify in court when the time came. Little did he know how his wish would later be granted.

CHAPTER 21
Black Jazz Found

THE SEARCH FOR Jazz continued, and now they had a general direction to look—north. Two hours later he was sighted, so they called Mark and Julie and told them to get their trailer and come get him. When the horse saw them, he nickered in recognition. He knew they were friends—not like that other man who'd hurt him.

Immediately, Jazz responded to Julie's whistle. As he got closer, she was shocked. Her beautiful horse was covered with welts. It looked like he'd been beaten with a belt or leather strap. She had tears in her eyes as she approached him. "Jazzy, you poor baby. What happened to you?" He nickered in response. When she touched the welts, he drew back in pain. "Easy boy, I won't hurt you. Just let me put this halter on you so we can get you home where you belong."

Jazz readily entered the trailer, then Mark drove slowly back to the ranch so the injured horse wouldn't be jostled any more than necessary. On their way back to Outfitters, Mark called their vet. "Dr. Vinson, this is Mark Hubbard. Please meet me at the ranch as soon as possible, and, yes, they found our horse."

When they arrived, the driveway was crowded with people, because they'd heard Jazz had been found. When Jazz was carefully backed out of the trailer, everyone gasped, not believing his condition.

They could clearly see he'd been abused by the man who had taken him. Julie slowly walked him to his stall.

***

After Bruce Nolan had been treated by the doctor, he was again questioned by Sheriff McKnight. He asked why they were talking with him again, because he'd already given his statement. "*I'm* the victim here. That horse was vicious and should be put away so no one else gets hurt."

He was informed that, thankfully, they'd found the missing horse but wanted to know why there were welts all over its body. He innocently responded, "I have no idea. The last time I saw him he was fine, and that was *after* he attacked me. I left as fast as I could, because I didn't know what else he'd do to me."

After another thirty minutes of questioning, he finally admitted he'd hit the horse a time or two but only because he was defending himself. He asked, "Who can fault me for that? It was self-defense. That beast may have killed me."

The sheriff shook his head. "Mr. Nolan, you keep changing your story. Now you say you fought back with your belt. Why didn't you say that in the beginning?"

Bruce became agitated and responded, "It shouldn't matter. That horse is a danger to everyone he encounters, and he should be put down."

Julie and her uncle were watching from behind the two-way mirror. Julie became furious. "He beat Jazz with a belt, and Jazz tried to protect *himself* the only way he could. How can that man lie like that? He has no shame. I hope no one believes him."

"Calm down, Julie. The sheriff knows the truth, and there *will* be consequences. He'll be put in prison for both stealing *and* abusing your horse. The story he told, and the timeline he gave, will never hold up in court, especially because he keeps changing it."

Julie murmured, "I hope so."

CHAPTER 22
Christmas Parade

BY THE END of summer, the riding center was up and running. In fact, it was booked solid, so Julie seldom got a chance to ride indoors. "Uncle Mark, we've created a monster." She laughed. "Everyone gets to use it but us."

"You need to get on the schedule, Jules. You own the place, don't you?"

She smiled. "I do, and I can hardly believe it." A few minutes later she asked her uncle if they could sit down and talk for a minute after dinner."

"What's on your mind?"

"I'll be ready to tell you tonight. It's just something I've been thinking about."

When they sat down to dinner, Mark said, "I'm not going to wait until *after* dinner. You tell me *now*."

Julie laughed. "Okay. I've been thinking we could have a Christmas parade, like they do before the rodeos. You know, where the parade ends up in the arena." She paused. "We can invite anyone who wants to participate, and I have some very special people in mind, if you think we can do it."

"Now you have my interest. Who might those special people be?"

"Do you remember how I wanted to create a therapeutic riding center for handicapped kids? Why can't we put those kids, and others from the area, in a wagon and pull them through town as part of the parade? We can get Shasta and Jazz used to a harness, and you know how snappy they would look—two beautiful, high-stepping, black Friesians pulling a wagon full of kids." She envisioned the scene in her mind. "I can see it now. What do you think?"

"Wow, Jules. That sounds like it would be great fun."

"Uncle Mark, don't you think even the special-needs kids would love it? I'm sure their parents would want to take a video of the whole thing, because their sons or daughters would be a part of a beautiful community event. We could even have Santa Claus set up in the arena so any kids who wanted to could sit on his lap. Wouldn't that be fun?"

"You've got quite an imagination, Julie. Estes Park usually has a Christmas parade, so maybe we could just become a part of it."

"Uncle Mark, you've lived here longer than I have, so will you suggest it to the town council?"

"I'd be glad to. And I'm sure the town would love to include us in their plans, especially since you have a booming business here now. Everyone in the area knows about the H-K Arena. It would be a wonderful opportunity for those who haven't seen it to go inside."

***

Jazz and Shasta were not happy when they were first strapped in their harnesses. It was a strange feeling, and Julie insisted on walking *behind* them instead of riding. After a while, they settled down, but the big test was hooking them to a wagon. Whoa! They didn't like that one bit! There was this *thing* chasing behind them. What if it caught up with them and scraped their hocks? After they understood the wagon wasn't going to run over them, they settled down. Though Julie and Mark were not riding them, they were still close by, which was reassuring.

To make it more fun, Julie attached leather straps of bells on their harnesses so they'd jingle when they walked, and jingle even more when they did their high-stepping trot. The horses loved the sound, and pulling the wagon wasn't hard work. It was just different.

Her uncle turned to her and smiled, and then he slapped the four reins lightly across the pair's back. "Let's get going. I want to see a little more speed from you two beasts." They responded immediately. He then leaned toward Julie, "See, they know I'm telling them I love them when I call them beasts."

Julie rolled her eyes. "Yeah, right. I'm sure they understand that."

***

The afternoon of the parade, Julie hooked several strands of battery-operated LED lights to their harnesses. The horses weren't at all sure they liked the colored lights, because some blinked. But, by the time the sun went down and the kids were loaded in back, the two horses were fine with the lights. In fact, the Christmas music and colorful floats excited them, so they pranced like fancy show horses.

Mark sat on the bench seat at the front of the wagon, and Julie faced backward to check on, and enjoy, the smiling passengers.

Snowflakes were starting to fall, and with the colored lights playing on their faces, the kids looked radiantly happy. Some of their moms and dads walked beside them taking pictures and laughing. Parents of the special-needs children were seldom able to share in gleeful, and wonderfully *normal*, activities with their children, and they knew the whole family would remember this night for a long, long time—both in their hearts and on film.

Many in the parade had no idea they were headed toward the H-K Arena. What a surprise it would be when the parade drove in and circled the arena three times while a band played carols, and people cheered. The overhead lights would be dimmed to make the beautiful colored lights on the floats seem even more colorful. At one end of the covered arena there was a small house. And who should be waiting for them but *Santa Claus!* He was eager to laugh with the kids and listen to what they wanted for Christmas. Both young and old lined up to see and talk with him, and then they slipped over to a table set up with Christmas goodies, cocoa, and hot apple cider, to fill their stomachs. The night was magical, and Julie was very proud to be a part of it!

When they got home and had the horses settled in for the night, Julie thought she'd be exhausted, but she was still excited and found it hard to sleep. Once in her bed her thoughts turned to God. *Father, you created an amazing night for this town and especially for those precious kids. Not just for those with special needs, but for all the kids. I saw no fussing or squabbling, just happiness and celebration. A chaplain said a prayer before Santa met with the children, so you were given your rightful place of honor. Again, I thank you for the wonderful evening and for a chance to remember and celebrate your son's birth. In Jesus's name I pray ... I mean praise ... Amen.*

Christmas came, and so did Jazzy's party. "Jazz, you are now four years old, which makes me almost fifteen. The four years I've been here have been the best of my life. I can't imagine what it would have been like if I had been forced to go back to Florida."

Uncle Mark walked in and heard the last two sentences. "Jules, they have been the best four years of my life as well. I never knew what I was missing until you came along, little girl. And about your living in Florida, you probably would've found a cute surfer boyfriend and forgotten all about Jazz."

"You know that's not true. My horse would have been there with me."

He added, "But we wouldn't have been there to celebrate his birthday."

She agreed and told him she didn't want to talk about Florida, because she loved her life the way it was here in Colorado.

CHAPTER 23
Black Jazz a Barrel Racer?

FALL THE NEXT year, the phone rang, and Julie turned to her uncle. "I wonder who that is? I would think everyone else would be celebrating Thanksgiving with their family." She picked up the phone. "Hello. Oh, it's you, Ruth."

She sounded distraught. "You know how fond I am of Dusty and Rex. I have some bad news. Dusty found Rex limping around his stall this morning. When he examined his leg, it was terribly swollen, so he called the vet, who gave Rex a shot and wrapped his leg. He told Dusty Rex must have cut himself on something, it festered, and now he can barely walk."

Julie was concerned. "I hope his horse will be okay."

"Eventually, he should be fine, but Dusty has a big competition coming up in three weeks, and now has no horse to ride."

"Ruth, that's terrible. I know how competitive he is, and how he loves to win those ribbons."

"Honey, it's not just ribbons he wins. Dusty is on the pro rodeo circuit, and that's how he makes his living. He's won enough events this year to qualify to barrel race in the National Finals Rodeo in December. Everyone knows the NFR is the richest rodeo on earth, with over $5 million at stake over the ten-day run.

By the end of the rodeo he could have won enough money to last through next year."

She continued. "Of course, placing first is almost impossible, but even placing third or fourth could net him a sizable chunk of money. He's been counting on doing well, but now Rex is not able to race."

Julie had been relaxed and happy, but the news about Dusty was depressing. "What can we do?"

Ruth hesitated a minute. "We can find him a good horse to ride. It's not just the horse that wins the race but also the rider and his skill. He just needs a good barrel racing horse."

Julie answered. "Uncle Mark has horses here, but not of Rex's quality."

Ruth threw out a suggestion. "How about Jazz? I know you've been practicing barrel racing on him, and his times are getting better."

"But, Ruth, he's not a barrel racing horse."

"Julie, Dusty *is* a barrel racer and a very good one. We all know it's not just the horse but the skill of the rider that really counts."

Julie shook her head. "I don't know. Dusty would only have three weeks to get Jazz ready."

"Honey, Dusty is desperate, and you've been working Jazz around the barrels. It's worth a shot, isn't it?"

She reluctantly agreed, and Ruth called him to tell him she had found a horse he could ride at the NFR.

Julie led her horse out when she saw Dusty enter the indoor arena. He hadn't known which horse Ruth had found for him to use, so he was shocked when he saw Jazz.

Julie, are you sure you want to loan him to me for this competition? You are the only one who's ever ridden him."

She responded, "Yeah, I know, but it couldn't be for a better cause—to help out a friend. I just don't know how much help he'll be. He's gotten pretty fast around the barrels, but I'm sure we haven't gotten close to the times you turn in."

Dusty reached up and patted Jazz's neck. "How ya' doin', big boy? You gonna let me ride you today?" Then he pulled himself up into the saddle, preparing himself for a buck or two. There was no reaction, so he leaned over and whispered in his ear. "Good boy. I think we'll get along fine."

With that, he gathered the reins, and they trotted around the barrels that had been set up in the arena. So far, so good. Jazz didn't resist him, but the true test would be when he urged him to gallop.

Julie called out, "Ready, set, go!" Dusty leaned forward and headed for the first barrel. He was surprised at how responsive Jazz was, and he was glad Julie had taken this past year to keep practicing the tight turns, because the training showed. He was not as fast as Rex, but he was eager. Fortunately, Dusty still had three weeks to refine the turns and get him in the best shape possible for the big competition.

After an hour, he pulled up beside Ruth and Julie. "I think he's going to be okay. He may not be as fast as Rex, but he seems to love cutting those barrels close. I think he'll make up some time that way. And Julie, I hope you don't mind if I spend lots of time with your horse, because he not only needs to keep cutting those corners tight, but we'll be practicing wind sprints to make sure he can put on speed when I ask him to."

She looked up at Dusty and grinned. "Why would I mind? This is free training for my horse. You can only make him better."

He looked down at her. "Thanks, Julie. I appreciate the use of Jazz, as well as your support. You'll be coming to the NFR when I compete, won't you? I know Las Vegas is pretty far from Estes Park, but I'd love to see you, Mark, and Ruth there. You'd be my personal cheering section. I'm sure Jazz would appreciate it too."

"We wouldn't miss it for the world. I'm just glad it won't conflict with our Christmas parade. We'd hate to miss that."

CHAPTER 24
The Competition

BEFORE JAZZ WAS led into the trailer headed to Las Vegas, Julie hugged his neck. "I know you've been working very hard, so I want your best when you get in the arena. Ruth, Uncle Mark, and I will be there cheering you on. Don't worry, you'll be easy to spot because I know you'll be the prettiest horse, and the only Friesian, in the event."

Dusty walked up to her and gave her a hug. "Thanks again, Jules. I think he's ready, and I know I am. That indoor arena of yours has been a lifesaver. Don't worry about Jazz, because I'll take good care of him." Then he turned, got in the truck, and pulled the trailer out of the drive.

***

"Ladies and gentlemen, first up is Gary Forbes on Sundance Delight. Let's welcome them, and watch 'em take the barrels." The horse and rider shot from the alleyway leading to the arena. They zipped around the course, but Sundance knocked over a barrel, which gave him "no time" for the round. Some rodeos add five seconds to a rider's time for a knockover, but the NFR had its own rules. The crowd cheered anyway, because, as the returning champion from last year, he'd been the favorite, and he still had more tries to keep his title.

"Next up is Randy Wright on Moon Walker. This pair did very well last year as well. Let's see if they can keep up their speed and get a clean round." The run was clean, but their time was a disappointing 19.7 seconds. "Folks, they'll have to do better than that to win this event. Remember, Gary Forbes won with an amazing 16.8 last year."

"Our third contestant will be Dusty Rhoads on Black Jazz. Dusty has done very well on the circuit this year, but this is Black Jazz's debut. Dusty's horse, Rex, is on the injured list. I don't believe we've ever seen a Friesian race the barrels at the NFR, so this should be interesting. When they enter the arena, give them a big hand."

Julie grabbed Mark's hand and shouted, "There he is! There's Jazz!" She prayed, *Lord, you know how much I love my horse. Make Dusty and Jazz do well, and above all, keep them safe.*

Horse and rider shot out of the alley and hit the electronic eye at full speed. They rounded the first two barrels with no problem but tipped the third one before racing back to the finish line.

Julie was dismayed. "I'm sure Dusty is upset because they didn't make good time, but at least he has more tries." She looked over at Ruth. "Does tipping a barrel add seconds to his time?"

Ruth answered. "No. Actually, in this particular rodeo there isn't a penalty for tipping a barrel, not even if the rider actually touches it to keep it from falling over. Personally, I've never seen a rider touch one."

The riders were all very good, which didn't surprise Julie. After all, this was the finals for the year. But she was surprised one rider was disqualified from the event because he ran out of rotation. She thought, *How could anyone forget the position they drew, especially if they knew they'd be disqualified if they started out of order?* But she was grateful he had.

At the end of the day, Gary Forbes on Sundance Delight took first in the barrel racing. Julie was disappointed Dusty and Jazz came in fourth, but she clapped anyway. She felt bad until they visited Dusty behind the arena. He was grinning from ear to ear.

"Dusty, aren't you upset you and Jazz didn't place higher?"

He explained why he was happy. "Julie, three weeks ago I had no horse to ride, and you offered me Jazz. We trained hard, and as you saw tonight, we did our best. Jazz is not a quarter horse, and his breed is not known for its speed, but he was crazy good around the corners."

"So you aren't disappointed?"

"Not in the least. Part of our fourth-place win was because one contestant was disqualified for riding out of rotation, and, frankly, some of the others had a *really* bad night. Their times were terrible. I was blessed with a horse with a willing heart, and Jazz and I took advantage of their bad luck."

He reached over and patted Jazz's neck. "I have a new respect for Friesians. They have big hearts and want to do whatever is asked of them, to the best of their ability. Think about it, we came in fourth out of all the horses racing the barrels. The NFR is not a rinky-dink rodeo, so only the best are allowed to come here, and your horse placed fourth. I can hardly believe it! I am tickled, and proud to have ridden him. Think of it this way. I won more money than I would have if I hadn't competed at all, so it was a win for me."

The next morning, Mark, Julie, and Ruth followed Dusty's trailer home. They made it in just under thirteen hours, because they'd only taken one break to eat, they gassed up a couple of times, and only one stop to let Jazz out to stretch his legs. They knew it was a long, hard trip, but they all wanted to get home and sleep in their own beds. When Julie put Jazz in his stall, she promised him a good brushing the next day. It wouldn't only be a treat for him, but for Julie too. She'd missed caring for him, because for a while it seemed like he had become Dusty's horse.

"Jazz, I'm so proud of you for working so hard for Dusty. Now when I work the barrels you can teach *me* what to do." He nickered and searched her pocket for treats.

As usual, they celebrated his birthday, but this time Dusty was there. He wanted Mark to take a picture of him, Jazz, and Julie with the ribbon they'd won.

EPILOGUE

Later that year, Julie took a few minutes to review her life since coming to Colorado. She had a beautiful horse named Black Jazz, a great dog named Brutus, new friends, her Uncle Mark was wonderful to her, and she was an asset to her community. But most of all, she had a renewed love for Jesus, and so had her Uncle Mark. Not bad for someone just coming up on her sixteenth birthday.

Julie had been devastated when her parents died in a plane crash. It crushed her heart and her world. In the end, the Lord made her life rich and fruitful because she'd come to love and trust in him.

She'd learned we can't even imagine what God has prepared for those who love him. She believed this with all her heart, because everything God had done for her was far beyond her wildest dreams, and she knew she was blessed.

DISCUSSION QUESTIONS

Have you had upsetting events in your life that made you move, change schools, or give up friends? How did you handle it?

How does having close attachments to pets and friends make your life easier? How does having a personal relationship with God make your life easier?

Explain how Julie's Christian faith began to show in her life. Who have you asked to attend church, and did they go with you? Did you discuss the experience with them later?

Have you ever blamed God, or other people, for bad things that have happened to you? Explain how Julie finally got over blaming her parents when they died. Have you ever asked God's help when you needed to forgive someone? How did he help you?

If you enjoyed this book, you might like to read
Shady Springs Ranch.

CHAPTER 1
Brielle's New Foster Home

"Brielle, I want you to realize you're being given another chance to have a normal life with a loving foster family. The Kellingtons are an older couple who lost their daughter three years ago, and now they've decided they want to take in and love another child."

There was a long pause with no response.

"You can't run away again. Do you understand that? No one wants to take a chance on being responsible for a child who constantly runs away."

Another long pause with no response.

"People who take on this responsibility also invest their hearts when they open up to love another child." Vicki Stone shook her head as she watched the wipers swish the rain off her windshield. She wished she could see inside the head of the young girl sitting beside her.

Brielle looked out the window as the car sped toward her new home. *No, not home*, she thought, *a new place*. She already knew she'd hate where she was going and would run away again. Maybe next time she wouldn't be found.

When they pulled into the driveway, the Kellingtons came out to greet them. They looked like they wanted to run toward the car, but they held each other back and slowed to a walk.

Brielle thought, *How lame*. She got out of the car and pulled her knapsack from the back seat. She didn't have much, but that meant there would be less to carry when she left. She wondered how long it would be before she grew tired of them and snuck out of the house late at night.

"Hi there, Brielle. Welcome to Wimberley, Texas. My name is Brenda Kellington, and this is my husband, Paul. Welcome to our home. We hope you'll like living here."

Vicki introduced herself to the Kellingtons and followed them up the porch steps. She then turned and looked out over the yard with its many pine trees and well-trimmed bushes. "Lovely place you have here. Brielle has always lived in the city, so this will be a good change for her." Then she turned around and entered the large and inviting log and stone home. She had always loved looking at houses, and this one was spectacular.

Brielle admired nothing and said nothing.

Once inside, Brenda turned and offered to get them iced tea and cookies if they were hungry. Vicki accepted the offer, but Brielle simply looked away and flopped down on the closest chair.

It was hard to make conversation with a person who refused to respond, but Vicki continued to talk as if she were getting answers. "Brielle, isn't this a lovely house? It's large and beautifully decorated. I think you'll like it here. I understand it's a working, cattle and horse ranch." There was a pause while she tried to think of something else to say. "Weren't those fences we saw on the way in pretty? And did you notice the horses in the pastures? You might like to go out to their stables later." She finally stopped trying to make conversation and quietly waited for the refreshments to be brought from the kitchen.

After the foster parent contract was signed, Vicki got up to leave. She leaned over and whispered to Brielle, "Remember what I said. This may be your last chance for a placement, and the Kellingtons seem to be a lovely couple. Give them and yourself a chance. This could be a wonderful place for you." She straightened up, turned, and walked toward the door, glancing back at the scowling young girl who had moved from the chair and was now sprawled out on the sofa. She silently offered up a prayer. *God, please give the Kellingtons the patience needed to break through Brielle's shell of indifference. Only You can turn this hateful and probably frightened young girl into someone loving and special. Help her see these people are being the hands and feet of Christ, offering to show her the way to a wonderful life of peace and contentment. Amen.*

After the door closed, Brenda turned to Brielle and offered her a hand. "Would you like to come upstairs with me to see your room?"

Brielle looked at her new foster mother's hand with disdain, then ignored it as she got up from the couch without help.

Brenda simply turned away and said, "Follow me."

Brielle followed but dragged her knapsack behind her, trying to make as much noise possible as they walked up the stairs.

Her room was beautiful. The walls were covered with a light wood paneling, and the floor was natural stone with thick rugs to take the chill off the feet on cold days. It even had an unusual wrought iron screen in front of the stone fireplace. She peered into the large bathroom, but said nothing. She'd never had a bathroom of her own, but she wasn't going to show them she was impressed. Besides, she wasn't going to stay anyway.

The four-poster bed was positioned so she could sit on her bed and look out the window at the Blanco River—not that it mattered. The beautiful quilt covering her bed was pieced together with muted fabrics, and the pillows lining the headboard were fluffed up, soft and full. When her new foster mother left, Brielle sat in a chair by the fireplace and stared into the fire that had been lit to warm her room. She refused to sit on the inviting bed. Tears filled her eyes when she imagined this home and family vanishing like all the others. She always left to avoid being tossed out, and she wondered how long it would be before she felt rejection again.

A tap on the door jolted her from those thoughts. She responded to the knock in a gruff voice, "What do you want?"

Brenda answered cheerily, "I just wanted to tell you we're eating in thirty minutes, so you'll have time for a quick shower."

She responded hatefully, "I don't want a shower."

"I'll come back and let you know when we're ready to eat."

"Suit yourself."

Brenda and Paul were making a salad and checking on the chicken roasting in the oven when Paul said, "Well, not a wonderful start, but we'll give her time. I just hope she allows herself to get to know us. It would be a shame if she cuts herself off from all the support and love we desperately want to give her."

Upstairs, a debate was going on. Brielle thought, *Should I stay up here and skip dinner to show them I don't care to be around them, or should I go down for dinner, eat, and run back up to my room?* Hunger won out. She could smell dinner cooking, and it had been quite a while since she'd had a home-cooked meal. Still wearing her old jacket, she slowly made her way downstairs, following the smell of food.

When she rounded the corner into the kitchen, Brenda said, "Hi! Glad you could join us."

Their cheerful attitude annoyed her, so she didn't respond. She would eat quickly and scoot back upstairs before they started asking her questions. There were always questions. She'd found that out.

As they were eating, Paul said, "Brielle, you're going to be living here, so if you'd like, you can call us Paul and Brenda instead of Mr. and Mrs. Kellington."

Brielle kept eating and didn't respond, but she thought, *Why should I call them Paul and Brenda? I'm going to be out of here soon anyway. I don't want them to think I'm getting friendly and fitting into their precious little family. If I keep calling them Mr. and Mrs. Kellington, they'll know I'm not going to let them sucker me into caring for them.*

Dinner was surprisingly pleasant. No questions were asked, and the only subject discussed was the horses they had on the ranch. As she was getting up to make her break, Paul said, "Brielle, since it's still light out, would you like to go down and see the horses?"

She hadn't expected that question. She shrugged and said, "Yeah, I guess." The talk of horses at the dinner table had made her curious, because she'd never even seen a horse up close.

CHAPTER 2
The Rescue Horse

Brielle could hear the horses before she saw them. Evidently, neighs, snorts, banging, and stomping hooves were common sounds when they were being fed. Very few heads poked out of the stalls at feeding time because they were busy chomping and crunching on their food. It gave her a chance to look into the stalls without some old horse poking its head out and trying to bite her. When she finally peeked in one, she thought, *Oh my! They're huge!* She would've run out of the barn if she hadn't felt protected by a heavy mesh half door between her and the horse.

Mrs. Kellington looked over at her. "Well, what do you think? Are horses what you expected?"

Brielle shook her head no and then asked, "I know people ride horses, but why would horses let them? They could stomp a person in a heartbeat and kill them."

Brenda responded, "For some reason, horses seem to like people, at least people who are nice to them. Big dogs could easily slash people with their sharp teeth, but they don't unless they're mistreated. I believe God knew humans would need friends, so He made horses and dogs for us to use and enjoy." She chuckled. "Dogs and horses are *very* different from cats. It appears God made humans to serve cats."

That got a small smile out of Brielle because she *did* have experience with cats.

Brenda then asked, "Would you like for me to take this horse out so you can get a better look?"

Brielle backed up and stammered, "No, that's okay. I can see it from here."

When she got back to her room, she thought about the horses and how big they were. Brenda had petted each horse, and none had tried to bite her. In fact, when she gave them each a slice of apple, they didn't lunge and grab it from her. They simply nibbled with their lips and gently lifted it from the palm of her hand. Maybe there was something to God making horses to serve humans. She knew most dogs were like that too. They loved people to pet them unless they'd been abused and taught to hate. She would have to think about that. Then she began to wonder if people were also like that ... rejecting people because they had been rejected ... or because they expected to be rejected.

The Kellingtons saw very little of Brielle over the next few days. She ate with them, but stayed in her room the rest of the time, curled up in a wingback chair by the fireplace, reading the many books she found there. She thought this may have been their daughter's room and these were her books. She must have loved to read, too.

Occasionally, Brenda knocked on the door and peeked in, gratified to find Brielle with her nose in a book. *Good,* she thought. *She loves to read like my Tammy.* Those thoughts always brought a tear or two because she had many good memories of her daughter.

When Brielle had exhausted the supply of books in her room, she asked Mrs. Kellington if she could look in the downstairs library for more. She was told she could. When she left the library, she was asked who had taught her to love reading.

That was another question she hadn't expected, so she answered without thinking. "My mom loved to read before she started doing drugs. She would say it was a way to take a trip without leaving the farm." Brielle was afraid there would be more questions, so she quickly scurried upstairs and shut the door. Had she said too much? Why had she shared that her mother was a drug addict? She could have kicked herself. Giving out that kind of information would certainly bring more questions, and she hated questions.

A week later, Brielle was awakened by noise in the driveway. She looked out her window and saw Mr. Kellington talking to a man who had just driven in pulling a horse trailer. He motioned for the man to drive over to the barn and told him to wait for him there. Mrs. Kellington joined him, and they both trudged after the trailer. Brielle was curious and wondered what she was missing. She quickly threw on her clothes and joined the procession. When she got close to the barn, she hid behind a bush so she could see what was going on without being seen. It wouldn't be good to let them know she was curious about something going on at the ranch.

Mr. Kellington called out, "Mac, let the ramp down slowly and back her out. We don't want to scare her any more than she is already." A very scraggly, reddish-brown horse was backed down the ramp into the yard. It didn't look *anything* like the other horses on the ranch. This one was very skinny, with a matted coat, and looked exhausted.

Mrs. Kellington took the lead rope and went to the horse's head, giving her a pat. "It's okay, girl. Things will be better now." The horse nuzzled her and nickered softly.

Brielle wondered, *Why was that old horse brought here?* When her curiosity got the better of her, she stepped out from behind the bush. "Good morning. I heard someone pull up and saw everyone heading toward the barn. What's happening?"

Everyone looked up at the sound of her voice, surprised she was out of bed since it was only seven o'clock in the morning.

Mr. Kellington answered, "We have a new horse here at Shady Springs Ranch."

"*That's* the name of this ranch?" With a distasteful note in her voice, she asked, "Why did you name it *that*? It's a weird name for a ranch."

Paul smiled, eager to explain some of the history of his ranch. "Shady Springs Ranch has been in my family for many years, and it's never occurred to me to change the name. I imagine it was given that name because we have many springs on the property, and the water from our springs is not only cool but cold. And of course the trees make it shady."

"Why is it cold?"

Paul was happy to continue his explanation. "There's an artesian spring under our land that gives us spring water." He paused. "To better answer your question, it's so cold because the water in the artesian spring is stored in underwater caves located deep in the ground under Wimberley, where the heat from the earth's surface doesn't reach it."

All Brielle could say was, "Oh ... if you say so." She quickly changed the subject with another question. "Why does that horse look so bad?" She had put her foot in it again.

Mrs. Kellington took no offense and answered the question with an explanation. "Several years ago, we heard about people who had lost their jobs or gotten sick and were unable to take care of their animals. There were cases where horses actually died from malnutrition because their owners couldn't feed them. We found several equine rescue organizations in the area that took these horses in when the owners were reported to animal control, so we contacted them to see how we could help. Believe it or not, many we have here at Shady Springs are rescue horses, which brings us to the horse brought in today. Several other horses found with this one had to be put down by the vet because they were too far gone, but this mare will probably make it with enough food and tender, loving care."

Brielle was amazed people actually cared about these dying horses, but she said nothing. She wondered what made people want to help animals ... and even kids. After lunch, she wandered in the direction of the stables, trying to act like the horses were not drawing her to them. She pitched a few pine cones in a nearby pond, then sat on a bench overlooking the creek that flowed into it. Finally, she stretched, then casually sauntered toward the horse barn.

Once inside, she peered in each stall, looking for the horse brought in earlier that day. It was behind the last door on the right. As she peeked over the door, she thought, *Poor thing.* It still looked a mess and didn't react when she clucked softly to get its attention. After several minutes, she slowly unlatched the stall door and made her way to the horse's head, watching to make sure it didn't turn and bite her. The horse didn't move, though she knew it had heard her. It just stared straight ahead into the dark corner of the stall. When she lightly touched its neck, its skin rippled as if trying to shake off a fly. The horse looked so pitiful it broke her heart. If only she had a bit of apple to offer. Surely it wouldn't bite if she gave it a treat. When she came out to the stable again, she'd have to remember to bring something horses liked to eat.

It looked like someone had brushed the mud from the horse's coat, but its fur was still dry and lifeless. When she moved closer, it turned its head toward her. Imagine her surprise when she saw warm, intelligent brown eyes looking at her. She didn't see fear or panic in them but curiosity. How could that be? This animal had been neglected and had almost died. She slowly held out her hand for it to sniff and was rewarded with a gentle puff of air.

She thought she'd be afraid if it made any sound at all, but she didn't even flinch. It was telling her she was accepted, and now they were friends.

Brielle thought a lot about the horse as she returned to the house. It occurred to her that she didn't even know if it was male or female. Earlier in the day, it had just been a poor, sad, ugly animal, and now they seemed to have a relationship ... a bond. She didn't understand how that happened, but she was sure it did.

CHAPTER 3
The Mistake

Brielle was quiet at supper that evening, because things seemed to be changing. She no longer hated the Kellingtons or wanted to leave, but she didn't want to talk about the change either. What would she say? That she suddenly felt something for a horse and she was beginning to learn nice things about the Kellingtons as well? How crazy was that? She would just keep quiet until she sorted it all out in her head. However, she did speak up and ask if the horse brought in that day was a male or female. They told her it was a mare—a female.

The next morning, Mr. Kellington ran in the house and yelled for his wife to call Dr. Rubin to come look at the new mare. Before Brielle could stop herself, she panicked and said, "What's wrong? What's wrong with the new horse? Is she going to be okay?" Paul and Brenda ran to the stable, and Brielle followed because she was worried. When they reached the barn, Brielle said, "She was fine yesterday afternoon. What could be wrong?"

They turned and asked her directly, "Were you out here yesterday afternoon?"

She responded defensively, "Yes. Why? I didn't do anything wrong."

Calmly, Paul asked, "Brielle, did you go in this horse's stall?"

"Yes, but was that wrong?"

Paul looked at his wife, then back at Brielle. "Did you make sure you latched the door when you left?"

She stammered, "I think so. It looked like it was closed."

He spoke to her gently. "Sweetheart, the door was unlatched … in fact open when I went to the barn this morning. We think she got out of her stall and found the door to the feed room open because the lid to the grain bin had been nudged off on the floor."

Brielle responded hotly, "What are you trying to tell me?"

Dr. Rubin rushed into the barn before Paul could explain and interrupted. "Paul, let's see that sick horse of yours." After a short examination of the mare lying in the straw, he said, "I know you know that horses that have been starved should not be fed a lot of food, especially rich grain. The amount of fluids they drink should also be limited because they tend to swill down their water when they're thirsty. What did this mare eat after I left here yesterday?"

Paul rubbed his neck and answered, "I don't really know. We restricted her food, but I believe she accidentally got out of her stall and probably made it into the feed room."

The kneeling vet looked up briefly while running his hands along the mare's belly. "From what I can see, and from what you've told me, she probably has colic. Horses that have been starved often bolt down their food and water and are at risk of becoming colicky, but fortunately, this one doesn't look too bad right now. It's also possible she was so hungry the last place she lived that she grabbed at whatever grass she could and accidentally ate dirt and sand with it. That wouldn't have been good for her either. I recommend you make sure she has clean food and water, and remember, feed her regularly and don't try to plump her up with larger than normal meals. Her stomach just can't take it."

Brielle asked, "Is she going to be okay?"

When the vet stood up, he smiled and reassuringly patted her on the back. "I think so. I've given her a shot of something that will help her feel better, and I recommend she also be given a supplement in her food. Now let's get her up and start walking her around. Sometimes that helps expel the gas that's causing the pain."

Brielle started toward the house before Dr. Rubin even left the barn. She knew she was going to be yelled at—or worse—when the Kellingtons came inside. She didn't mean to hurt the horse, but she knew she was to blame because she didn't make sure the lock was fastened when she left the afternoon before.

Brielle heard them enter the house and began trembling when she heard them coming up the stairs. The door opened, and they both walked in. Brenda Kellington held out her arms and took her hands. "Oh, Brielle, I'm sure you feel terrible about not making sure the stall door was latched, but it was just a mistake … not done on purpose. In this house, we're not punished for our mistakes. We learn from them." She looked over at her husband and smiled. "Why don't we all go downstairs and have a big breakfast, because I'm starved."

Relief flooded over Brielle, and she responded, "If you don't mind, I'll be down in a minute." When they left, she fell on her bed, relieved the mare was going to be okay and shocked that the Kellingtons hadn't yelled at her for being so stupid. Tears silently slipped down her cheeks. Where did that emotion come from? She hadn't cried in years. Before going to the kitchen, she got up and quickly splashed water on her face, then combed her hair and put on clean clothes. When she first arrived at Shady Springs, it hadn't mattered if they liked her or not, because she knew she was leaving them anyway. Now, she wasn't so sure.

When Brielle walked in the kitchen, she looked different. Her thick auburn curls were pulled back in a pretty headband, and she looked clean and fresh. Even more surprising, she was smiling. Brenda and Paul looked at each other and shrugged. It was the first time they'd seen her look happy, and they were delighted.

That evening, the Kellingtons prayed, "Father, You tell us to praise You in all things. We know You didn't cause colic in our new horse, but You did give us a wonderful opportunity to show Brielle our love and grace. I don't think she expected to be forgiven for a mistake that caused that mare pain. When we saw the smile on her face after our little talk, we knew You were working Your magic in her heart. Thank You again for the opportunity to show her our love and to model the forgiveness You expect us to give others. Amen."

Printed in the United States
By Bookmasters